John Dryden, Geoffrey Chaucer, May Estelle Cook

Palamon and Arcite

The Knight's Tale

John Dryden, Geoffrey Chaucer, May Estelle Cook

Palamon and Arcite
The Knight's Tale

ISBN/EAN: 9783337090005

Printed in Europe, USA, Canada, Australia, Japan

Cover: Foto ©Andreas Hilbeck / pixelio.de

More available books at **www.hansebooks.com**

The Lake English Classics

PALAMON AND ARCITE

OR THE KNIGHT'S TALE

FROM CHAUCER

BY

JOHN DRYDEN

EDITED FOR SCHOOL USE

BY

MAY ESTELLE COOK, A.B.
INSTRUCTOR IN ENGLISH, SOUTH SIDE ACADEMY, CHICAGO

CHICAGO

SCOTT, FORESMAN AND COMPANY

1898

CONTENTS

PREFACE

This edition of Palamon and Arcite aims to give the pupil only such information and stimulus as will enable him to do his best work. The notes have been prepared in the belief that stimulus to literary appreciation is quite as necessary to the young student as the understanding of facts, and have therefore been made suggestive as well as critical. The unique feature of the edition, that of footnotes from Chaucer's text, has been introduced in the hope that comparative study will not only add zest to the pupil's work, but will give him a basis for forming opinions of his own, and will consequently foster keenness of insight and power of enjoyment.

The text of Dryden used is that of W. D. Christie (Macmillan, 1893), the Chaucer text, that of Morris and Skeat's *Prologue* and *Knightes Tale* in the Clarendon Press Series.

M. E. C.

INTRODUCTION

CHAUCER

In the year 1340,* six years before the battle of Crécy, there was born in London a child who was destined to perpetuate in English the stories of chivalry. At Crécy, where cannon were used for the first time in European warfare, there appeared a force which was bound finally to destroy chivalry; for neither Norman castles nor Norman armor could withstand the power of firearms. But that result was long in coming about. Throughout the reign of Edward III. the fashion of chivalry was at its height; the ideal warrior was still the knight with "crested morion" and the lady's favor on his sleeve. Moreover, the English mind, which is often a little slow in its appreciation of the artistic value of things, had not until the fourteenth century wakened to the fact that the knight was not only a warrior, but also a fit subject for song and story. Englishmen, especially those who had been on the crusades, began to long for tales of knightly deeds, such as were already being sung by the poets of France and Italy. The time was

---

* This date is not definitely settled, but Chaucer's birth was certainly nearer 1340 than the traditional 1328.

ripe therefore for a master poet who would tell those same stories, and others, in the English tongue. That master poet came in the person of Geoffrey Chaucer.

Chaucer was happy in having not only a poet's power and a poet's opportunity, but also in living at the court of Edward III., the very heart of the English life of the fourteenth century, and being worldly wise in the interesting fashions of the times. It was a time of strange contrasts, when the romance of feudalism was jostling against the prosaic good sense of a growing business world, and the struggle between them was not yet decided. Chaucer was involved in both sides of the struggle in a way which to us seems almost contradictory, but which at the time was quite possible and natural; he was both a romancer and a man of affairs, and scarcely more the one than the other.

At sixteen or seventeen he became a page to Elizabeth, Duchess of Clarence, the wife of Lionel, son of Edward III., and from that time on he was all his life more or less actively engaged in the service of the royal family. Perhaps it was while he was a page, in the intervals of running errands and polishing armor, that he began to turn his reading to account by putting into his own words the stories he read; for we know that even then he was an omnivorous reader, and nothing could be more natural than that he should have entertained the other pages, and even the young princes, one of whom, John of Gaunt, was about his own age, with the recital of wonderful tales from Ovid or the French romancers. But whatever the reason was, the young Chaucer soon became a favorite with the court. He went with the army to France in 1359, and when taken prisoner was ransomed by no less a person than the king himself. To be sure, the king paid less for the freedom of the young poet than he paid the next day for a good horse; but that fact did not prove that he held his servant in slight regard, for he soon took Chaucer into his own service, spoke of him as *"dilectus valettus noster,"* and granted him a pension and a gift of clothes every Christmas. Chaucer married a maid of honor who was a namesake of the good Queen Philippa, the wife of Edward III.

He rose steadily in royal favor, holding several important positions, among them that of Comptroller of Customs for the port of London; in this position he was obliged to make the "rolls,"— that is, the bills and accounts,—with his own hand, a task which was no easy one, and the accomplishment of which proved him a competent business man. He was sent abroad on many important missions, such as negotiating treaties, and arranging for the marriage of the Black Prince's son, who afterwards became Richard II. There is a tradition, but no real proof, that on one of these journeys (1372-3) he visited Boccaccio at Florence and Petrarch at Padua. In 1386 he sat in Parliament as a knight of the shire from Kent. For a time after Edward III. died, and while John of Gaunt, Duke of Lancaster, who was Chaucer's patron and especial friend, was away from England, Chaucer lost his offices, and became acquainted with the sorrows of poverty and neglect. But perhaps he needed that experience to show him all sides of life. In any event his greatest poverty did not last long, for Richard II. remembered his early services and gave him an office. When John of Gaunt's son came to the throne as Henry IV. he promptly granted his father's friend a comfortable pension; so that before Chaucer died in 1400 he was happy in the certainty of his sovereign's favor. He was the first person buried in the Poet's Corner of Westminster Abbey.

All through his long life, Chaucer was reading and writing. He re-told many French and Italian romances, but always, as Shakspere did, in a way that made them thoroughly English in tone; for he borrowed only the thread of the story, often changing even that to suit his fancy, and making the details, the words, and the turn of thought new. One of his early long poems was the *Boke of the Duchess*, written in honor of John of Gaunt's first wife, who died in 1369. A little later he wrote what he called his "little tragedy" of *Troilus and Cresseide;* about the same time he made his first version of *The Story of Palamon and Arcite*. Another long poem, called the *Legende of Good Women*, he wrote at the queen's request, to make up for some of the sarcastic things he had said about women in his early poems; next to the *Canterbury Tales* it was his best work. The *Canterbury Tales*, a collection of twenty-four stories, was begun about 1388; and upon this poem, which was his masterpiece, Chaucer spent a large share of the last twelve years of his life.

Chaucer himself must have been a pleasant man to know. From passages scattered through his poems we suppose that he was short and plump, that he was "small and fair of face," that he had a shy, "elfish" look, that he usually carried his head bent forward and looked on the ground "as he would find a hare," and that his eyes were dazed with hard reading. He is pictured with a forked beard, "wheat color" when he was young and gray when he was not yet old, and with a dark gown reaching to his feet and an ink-horn at his side. Chaucer loved books, and perhaps was thinking of himself when he said of the Clerk:

> For him was levere[1] have at his beddes heed
> Twenty bokes, clad in blak or reed
> Of Aristotle and his philosophye,
> Than robes riche, or fithele,[2] or gay sautrye.[3]

---

[1] liefer, i. e. rather; [2] fiddle; [3] a psaltery, a musical instrument, something like a harp.

But better than books he loved the "softe, smalle, swote (sweet) grass," and his idea of happiness was to lie on the grass of a May morning and watch a daisy open to the sun. It seems to us now, as we go back to him after reading the poetry of the nineteenth century, that he was curiously limited in his appreciation of nature, for he never mentions the sea nor the sky nor the mountains; but the meadows and flowers and birds, to which his eyes were open, he speaks of with a simplicity and tenderness which we do not find again until we read the lines of Burns and Wordsworth. Chaucer loved men and women, too. Although he lived among courtiers and princes, he did not scorn millers and ploughmen. He looked at people through very keen eyes, and laughed at their foibles, but without bitterness. He was reticent and quiet in manner, but in spite of that fact his enjoyment of all sorts of society was genuine. One can easily imagine him sitting among a chance company of travelers such as he describes in the *Canterbury Tales*, seeing and hearing everything without appearing to watch any one, laughing quietly to himself now and then, saying never a word until he was called upon to speak, and then telling a better story than any of the company had ever heard before.

Besides making many French and Italian stories available in English, and adding to them not a few stories of his own, Chaucer did another good

service for English literature, and indeed for all
English speaking people. Before the reign of
Edward III. there was no literary language in
England which really deserved the name of English. Since the time of William the Conqueror
the Norman kings and their followers had gone on
speaking Norman-French, while the conquered
Anglo-Saxons had held to their own tongue. The
two languages had been coming nearer together all
the time, as the two peoples gradually became one
nation. But it was not until the time of Edward
III. that the new language, made of the union of
Norman and Anglo-Saxon, became the speech of
the nation. None of the deeds of the great
Edward are more worthy of remembrance than that
he decreed that English should be the language
of court and school. Norman courtiers had to
learn English, no matter how much they preferred
French; and school-boys from that time on translated their Latin exercises into English. The
writers who wished to be widely read must write
in English; accordingly Langland wrote his
Piers the Plowman in English, and Wyclif translated the Bible into English. But the language
of both Langland and Wyclif was crude and
rugged; it was like a hard path, full of jagged,
unbroken stones. It was Chaucer who proved first
that English, in the hands of a master, might be
smooth-flowing and musical. The manuscripts of
Wyclif's Bible were being made while Chaucer

was writing the *Canterbury Tales*, but to us now it seems as though Wyclif's work might be a hundred years or more older than Chaucer's because his language is so much more primitive, so much less finished than Chaucer's. It is for this reason that the period of modern English literature is often dated from Chaucer. Granted that his manner is antiquated, that his words often need translation, it is still true that most of his lines are intelligible to us, and that as much cannot be said of any other writer of his time. For his modernness, as well as the beauty of his language, his pupil Lydgate called him the "load-star of our language," Spenser said he was "the well of English undefiled," and Tennyson sang of him as "Dan Chaucer, the first warbler."

DRYDEN

The life of the seventeenth century, in spite of the great stir made by the wars of Roundheads and Cavaliers, seems less romantic to us than that of the fourteenth century, though perhaps not rightly so. In the same way, and with more reason, the life of Dryden appears much more prosaic than that of Chaucer. Dryden was born in 1631, in the parish of Aldwinkle, Northampton. There he lived the ordinary life of an English boy of good family, studying, visiting, and fishing—a sport for which he never lost his fondness. When he was thirteen there was a day of excitement at his

father's house, when a force of Parliamentarians
barricaded themselves in the church hard by, and
were captured and imprisoned by a force of Royal-
ists.   But it is probable that young Dryden was
away at school at the time; certainly he never
referred to the event in his writings.   He prepared
for the university at the famous school in Westminster, where he was a favorite with the master,
Dr. Busby, and where he wrote good Latin exercises
and his first English verse.   He took his degree at
Cambridge in 1654 and then stayed at the university
until 1657, for farther study.   From Cambridge
he went to London, where he soon became famous.
In 1663 he married Lady Elizabeth Howard; but
tradition says, whether truly or not, that the
marriage was not a happy one.   For a time he
held a position which Chaucer had held, that of
Comptroller of Customs for the port of London;
but in his case the position was never more than
an honorary one, and probably even the pay was not
very regular.   In 1670 Dryden was made poet
laureate and royal historiographer, with a salary
of £200.   Even before this time he had become
the literary king of London, and the loyal followers who gathered about him of an evening at
Will's Coffee House took his slightest word as final,
whether he spoke of the latest news or of politics
or of the drama of the day or of literature in
general.   Scott gives an interesting, though of
course largely imaginary picture of him and his

court, in *The Pirate* (Chapter XIV). During
most of his life, Dryden allowed his politics, and
his religion also, to be decided by the party in
power. Under the Commonwealth he was a
Puritan, under Charles II. he was a Royalist and
a member of the Established Church, and under
James II. he became a Catholic. When the Prot-
estant William and Mary came to the throne,
however, he refused to change his faith again, and
lost his position as poet laureate in consequence.
Then, like Chaucer, he became acquainted with
neglect and comparative poverty. But he set himself to meet his misfortunes with hard work, and
wrote industriously and successfully until his death
in 1700. He was buried between Chaucer and
Cowley in Westminster Abbey.

It is almost impossible to think of Dryden's writings apart from his life. More truly than of
almost any other poet it might be said of him that
his work was his life. Moreover, most of Dryden's
poems were "occasional" pieces, written to celebrate some event in which he was interested either
by his own choice or by the king's wishes. The
poem which brought Dryden into notice and made
him decide on literature as a profession was the
Heroic Stanzas, written in praise of Cromwell at
the time of the great Protector's death. When
Charles II. came to his father's throne, Dryden
was ready with praise for him also, and wrote the
Astræa Redux (Justice Returned) to celebrate the

young monarch's return. With the Restoration
came a revival of the drama, and Dryden, always
ready to turn his hand to the need of the hour,
began to write plays. At first he wrote comedies,
but they went badly. With tragedies he had better
success, though as we read his plays now we think
it must have been the perverted taste of the
audience or the elaborate stage setting—in one play
there were singing angels and a vision of Paradise
—that carried them through. But these plays,
most of which were written in rhyme, did good at
least in the matter of training Dryden to use his
tools; for when the time came for his satires and
didactic poems, he had become a master of the art
of versification. In 1666 he wrote the *Annus
Mirabilis*, a poem which celebrated the wars with
Holland and the Great Fire of London. The
occasion of his first satire, called *Absalom and
Achitophel*, was the Popish plot. In this poem
the poet undertook the defense of the king against
Shrewsbury—Achitophel—and the excuse of the
Duke of Monmouth—Absalom. *The Religio Laici*,
Dryden's next important poem, has been called the
greatest English didactic poem; it was written in
a moderate and apparently sincere spirit of approval
of the views of the Church of England. Dryden's
last long poem, *The Hind and the Panther*, was
written after the accession of James II., and is an
allegorical defense of the Roman Catholic Church
under the symbol of the snow-white hind, against

the attacks of the English Church, which is symbolized by the spotted panther. When Dryden lost his position as laureate he again wrote plays. Most of his plays, both early and late, were adaptations of Shakspere or Molière or other dramatists, or dramatizations of popular stories; he even composed an opera, using *Paradise Lost* as a basis. Of his dramas the best are *All for Love* and *Don Sebastian*. Late in life Dryden undertook translations also. He translated Vergil, and passages from Homer, Theocritus, Ovid, Horace and Lucretius. His last undertakings were his book of *Fables*, which contained modern renderings of Chaucer, translations from Ovid and Boccaccio, and the second *St. Cecilia Ode*, which is usually called *Alexander's Feast*. Dryden's prose writing was always subordinate to his poetry, and consisted of prefaces to his poems or defenses of them. His chief essay, that on dramatic poetry, is an attempt to prove that rhyme is suitable for tragedy. His prose style has, however, stood the test of time better than his poetic style, because it is clear, simple, and direct.

Early in his career, when Dryden felt called upon to explain his failure as a writer of comedies, he said of himself: "My conversation is slow and dull, my humour saturnine and reserved; in short, I am none of those who endeavour to break jests in company, and make repartees." Perhaps in this confession Dryden was a little too hard on himself;

but he doubtless told more than a half-truth. There have been many conflicting opinions about his character. The truth of the matter seems to be that, living as he did in the unimaginative last half of the seventeenth century, when men made too much of their reason and valued too lightly warmth of heart, Dryden was rather too cold and practical. He was in danger of caring more for an argument than for the man who made it, and more for a well-turned line than for the moral effect of the idea it expressed. He lived a life too narrowly literary. He did sometimes go to the country for a short visit; but he was usually hard at work in London, he never went abroad, and he never saw life except through the eyes of a writer and critic. Wordsworth says that "there is not a single image from nature in all of Dryden's works," and while that criticism is not literally true, as some half dozen lines in *Palamon and Arcite* testify, it is true that Dryden did not love nature well enough to break away from the literary conventionalities of his time. He was not "saturnine;" but he was rather cold and stiff, and not so frank and joyous and responsive to the world and the people in it as Chaucer was.

Dryden must not, however, be criticised too severely. He lived in the beginning of the "classic age" of English literature, when it was the fashion to study Homer and Vergil rather than life, and to imitate the classics rather than to write new verses that should be truer than the classics to modern life. The result was inevitable; there was an artificial standard for literature, and people did not ask of a new poem "Is it true?" but "Is it like the classics?" Dryden, certainly, was partly responsible for setting this fashion; but he also, in part, merely reflected his age. If he was a trifle cold he was full of manly vigor and enterprise; if he was sometimes coarse he was always witty and workmanlike; if he did not study very closely the feelings of the human heart he did study the workings of the human mind, and leave us a fairly clear record of the thought of his day.

THE STORY OF PALAMON AND ARCITE

The story of Palamon and Arcite is the first one told by Chaucer in the series of stories called the *Canterbury Tales*. In the *Prologue* of the *Canterbury Tales* Chaucer tells how twenty-nine pilgrims spend the night at the Tabard Inn in Southwark on their way to the shrine of St. Thomas à Becket at Canterbury, and how, as they start out together the next morning, they agree to enliven the journey by telling stories. As the company is a motley one, including a knight, a squire, a yeoman, a prioress, a monk, a friar, a merchant, a clerk (student), a sergeant of law (lawyer), a franklin (country gentleman), a haberdasher, a doctor, a ploughman, a miller, and several other people, the stories are of very different sorts and are told in very different fashions. Some of them, indeed, Chaucer feels called upon to apologize for; not so for this first one, which is told by the knight, who naturally speaks first because of his social position. Chaucer calls the story simply *The Knightes Tale*. The knight himself is represented as having just come home from the crusades and as still wearing a buff jerkin stained with the wear of his armor; accordingly this tale of chivalrous devotion and knightly deeds comes appropriately from his lips.

The origin of the story of *Palamon and Arcite* is not known. It is quite possible that it was told at first as an independent story, and was afterwards connected with the name of Theseus, because this name was a favorite subject of romance, and came to be used in many legends which did not originally belong to Theseus himself. However that may be, it was taken from the Latin poet Statius by Boccaccio, who elaborated it in his *Teseide* into a poem of ten thousand lines. In Boccaccio's hands it has all the characteristics of a medieval tale; for example, the prayers of Emily and the two knights before the tournament are personified, and are sent to the gods to make the requests in person, while after the tournament the story follows Arcite's soul in its journey to heaven. Chaucer's version is not simply a translation, but rather a working-over so complete as to produce an almost original story; he reduces the poem to two thousand two hundred and fifty lines, makes the characters much more vivid and real, and the story itself more probable, and therefore more modern in tone. Dryden again expands the poem by nearly two hundred lines. His version is a much closer translation of Chaucer's than Chaucer's is of Boccaccio's; but Dryden did not scruple to change the lines decidedly when he saw fit. Dryden follows Chaucer, however, in giving the story an English setting. Inasmuch as Chaucer's knowledge of Greek life was very meager, his version is full of anachronisms, chief among which is the impossible term "Greek chivalry." But as there is no evidence that such a person as Theseus ever lived and as therefore the story is not a good subject for historical study, the fault is not a grievous one.

DRYDEN'S STYLE

However interesting it might be for the pupil to make a careful comparison of the styles of Chaucer and Dryden, it would scarcely be possible for him to do so with nothing more of Chaucer's poem at hand than the meager passages given in the footnotes. Those passages may well serve, however, to bring out by contrast the more important qualities of Dryden's style.

The basis of versification is the same in Chaucer and Dryden. Both poets write in heroic couplets, that is, in iambic pentameter, the lines rhyming in pairs. Such verse is peculiarly likely to be monotonous, and both poets show skill in varying the rhythm. Dryden sometimes substitutes a trochee or a spondee for an iambus, as in the lines:

Marching | he chanced | to cast | his eye | aside. |
and

Waked, as | her cus- | tom was, | before | the | day. |

He occasionally adds a foot; this iambic hexameter line is called an Alexandrine:

Two youth- | ful knights | they found | beneath | a load | oppressed. |

He also occasionally rhymes three successive lines (V. l. 31, 163, 183, etc.).

Dryden's rhyme, which, like Chaucer's, is often imperfect, is better than it seems to us, because the seventeenth century pronunciation made many words sound alike which are not alike in modern pronunciation. For instance, *joined* was pronounced *jined*, and the couplet

By fortune he was now to Venus trined,
And with stern Mars in Capricorn was joined,

was a perfect one. After this allowance is made, however, the fact remains that Dryden's rhyming is often careless.

Dryden's verse is more regular than Chaucer's, and at the same time less musical. It is like music played to metronome time, while Chaucer's is like music controlled by the player's

sense of rhythm. For this monotony of effect
one reason is that a large proportion of Dryden's
sentences are divided into clauses a line long;
accordingly, the pause in reading and the pause
in meter coincide, the voice falls at the end of
the line, and the time-beat becomes too notice-
able. For an illustration of the relief which
comes from carrying the thought of one line over
into the next, compare the following passages:

Dryden, l. 545—
It hăp- | pĕnĕd ōnce | thăt slūm- | bĕrīng ăs¹ | hĕ lāy, |
Hĕ drēamt | (hĭs drēam | bĕgān | ăt brēak | ŏf dāy), |
Thăt Hēr- | mĕs o'ēr | hĭs hēad | ĭn āir | ăppēarĕd, |
Ănd wĭth² | sŏft words | hĭs drōop- | ĭng spĭr- | ĭts
    chēerĕd. |

Chaucer, Knight's Tale, l. 525—
Ăt Thē- | bĕs, ĭn¹ | hĭs cŏn- | trēe ăs² | Ī sēyde, |
Ŭpōn | ă nĭght | ĭn slēep | ăs hĕ³ | hĭm lēyde, |
Hĭm thōughte | hŏw thăt⁴ | thĕ wĭn- | gĕd gōd | Mĕrcū-
    | rie
Bĭfōrn | hĭm stŏod, | ănd băd | hĭm tŏ⁵ | bĕ mūr- | ye.

The voice naturally joins the phrase "Biforn
him stood" with the preceding line, and thus
prevents the sing-song effect which Dryden's lines
have. The same extracts illustrate well a second
reason for the greater monotony of Dryden's
rhythm, namely, that the metrical stress in Dryden's line falls more often upon a syllable that

must be accented in reading, and that the time-beat within the line can therefore be disregarded less often than in Chaucer's line. The syllables which bear a metrical accent that may be passed over in reading are numbered in the two passages, and it is worthy of remark that there are only two in Dryden's lines, against five in Chaucer's.

In their choice of words Dryden and Chaucer differ widely. Dryden believes in the literary value of fine phrases, Chaucer in the appropriateness of simple words. Where Chaucer says that Palamon "caste his eye upon Emelya," Dryden says that he "descried the charms of Emily"; where Chaucer tells how Theseus "let Arcite out of prison," Dryden tells how Theseus "restored Arcite to liberty"; where Chaucer speaks of Theseus's "giving Arcite gold," Dryden speaks of Theseus's "largely entertaining Arcite with sums of gold." Dryden even occasionally sacrifices clearness or definiteness to an alliteration or a play upon words, as, for example, in the phrase "full of museful mopings," and the line,

Beholds whate'er he would but what he would behold

Dryden's diction often lacks the best artistic quality, therefore, because it lacks naturalness. On the other hand it has interest for the scholarly reader because many words which we now use only in their derived meanings are used by Dryden in their literal meaning.

Both Chaucer and Dryden often use long, loose sentences, and sometimes fail to make subordinate clauses depend grammatically upon principal clauses (V. 1. 304 and 786). Dryden also occasionally forgets that he has begun a dependent clause, and goes on with it as though it were principal (V. 1. 886). A marked characteristic of Dryden's style is the frequency of the balanced sentence. The setting of phrase against phrase, clause against clause, was not a new fashion in Dryden's time; but there was an epigrammatic, witty flavor in this style of writing which appealed to Dryden, and he fell into the habit of using it constantly, thereby establishing a fashion which was followed and carried to the extreme by Pope.

The first quality of Dryden's style which impresses the reader, and indeed which explains nearly every adverse criticism which can be passed upon it, is its lack of simplicity. Not only are his words pretentious in sound, but he sees his thoughts on their large and pompous side. There is a greater difference than a difference in wording between Chaucer's "ther is a noyse of peple" and Dryden's "The people rend the sky with vast applause." Chaucer is never afraid of a simple idea, nor of a homely one, if it is clear and pat. He says that Arcito "wex lene, and drye as is a shaft," and that his "disposicioun is turned al up-so-doun"; Dryden trims the thoughts up, as well as the phrases, saying that Arcite

> looks as wan
> As the pale spectre of a murdered man.

This lack of simplicity runs into such exaggerations as are expressed in

> Heaven is not but where Emily abides
> And where she's absent, all is hell besides,

and many similar passages. Another phase of the same quality shows in the over-emphasized, strained effect of such lines as

He swells with wrath; he makes outrageous moan;
He frets, he fumes, he stares, he stamps the ground.

These lines destroy sympathy because they try too hard to excite it. Dryden's artificiality, which comes out in his treatment both of nature and of people, is only another proof of his failure to take the world simply and naturally. There is much more feeling for Chaucer's favorite month in the three words "faire, fresshe May" than in Dryden's elaborate reference to the month when "Nature's ready pencil paints the flowers." In the same way there is an eye to literary effect rather than to Arcite's real love for Emily when the dying knight is made to say

> I feel my end approach and thus embraced
> Am pleased to die.

Chaucer's line

> And softe tak me in your armes tweye
> For love of God.

has the real pathos which Dryden's lacks.

Dryden is much less specific than Chaucer. Chaucer tells the color of Emily's hair, the age of King Emetrius, the exact hour at which Palamon goes to the temple of Venus. Not only does Dryden pass over such realistic details, but when he expresses the same thought that Chaucer does, he gives it in less pointed form. He is impersonal and general where Chaucer is personal and definite. In Chaucer, Arcite's comfort to Palamon has to do only with the two knights themselves:

> So stood the heven when that we were born;
> We moste endure it: this is the short and pleyn.

while in Dryden the sentiment applies to the whole world:

> Whate'er betides, by Destiny 'tis done;
> And better bear like men than vainly seek to shun.

Moreover, Dryden adds many generalizations which do not occur in Chaucer, such as,

> The proverb holds, that to be wise and love
> Is hardly granted to the gods above,

and,

> Law is to things which to free choice relate;
> Love is not in our choice, but in our fate.

Such sweeping statements enlarge the background of the poem, but at the expense of reality and vividness.

The fact that Dryden's poem is nearly two hundred lines longer than Chaucer's is proof that Dryden cannot tell a story as concisely as Chaucer. He has the power of condensed phrasing—witness such expressions as "Creon old and impious," "the woful captive kinsmen," the Creator's "all-seeing and all-making mind,"—but not of compact narrative. In the first place he wrote hurriedly, with little revision, and in the second place he was not content to let words suggest thoughts, but felt bound to state explicitly each phase of his idea. For example, in the extract given for scanning (l. 545), Chaucer, whose first line is merely introductory, tells the story of Arcite's dream in three lines where Dryden takes four.

In spite of the many points in which Dryden's style falls short of the ideal, it has a stateliness which commends it. His language is stiff and artificial; yet it was the accepted literary language of his time, and reminds us, not ungratefully, of that day of powdered wigs, velvet coats, artful conversations, and courtly manners. Chaucer's writing is quaint, simple, light-hearted, unconventional, full of wit and humor; Dryden's is purposely learned, serious almost to heaviness, lacking in humor, and only laboriously witty. Chaucer is spontaneous, as though he wrote for the love of writing; Dryden is premeditated, as though he wrote for fame and money. Nevertheless, Dryden is a literary workman "who needeth not to be ashamed," and is not altogether unworthy of

Doctor Johnson's praise that "Dryden found English poetry brick and left it marble."

DRYDEN'S ESTIMATE OF CHAUCER

Dryden called Chaucer the "Father of English Poetry," and spoke of him as a "perpetual fountain of good sense." The following extract from the introduction to the *Fables* is interesting because it not only gives Dryden's opinion of Chaucer, but also his reason for rewriting Chaucers' poems:

Chaucer, I confess, is a rough diamond, and must first be polished, ere he shines. I deny not likewise, that, living in our early days of poetry, he writes not always of a piece; but sometimes mingles trivial things with those of greater moment. Sometimes, also, though not often, he runs riot, like Ovid, and knows not when he has said enough. But there are more great wits besides Chaucer, whose fault is their excess of conceits, and those ill sorted. An author is not to write all he can, but only all he ought. Having observed this redundancy in Chaucer (as it is an easy matter for a man of ordinary parts to find fault in one of greater), I have not tied myself to literal translation; but have often omitted what I judged unnecessary, or not of dignity enough to appear in the company of better thoughts. I have presumed further, in some places, and added somewhat of my own where I thought my author was deficient, and had not given his thoughts their true lustre, for want of words in the beginning of our language. And to this I was the more emboldened, because (if I may be permitted to say it myself) I found I had a soul congenial to his, and that I had been conversant in the same studies.

SUGGESTIONS TO TEACHERS

This edition of *Palamon and Arcite* differs from previous ones in giving more of the Chaucer text, and in emphasizing the fact that the poem is more Chaucer's than Dryden's. The teacher is urged to belittle the difficulty of reading Chaucer, to take it for granted that the pupil can read the footnotes readily, and to add to the interest of the poem by making as full a comparative study as possible of the two poems. If the teacher is not familiar with the pronunciation and the grammar of Chaucer, he will find adequate directions for the pronunciation in Volume I. of the Riverside Edition of Chaucer's works, for the grammar in Morris and Skeat's edition of the *Prologue* and *Knightes Tale*, etc. (Clarendon Press Series.) The pleasure of his pupils in hearing Chaucer well read will amply repay him for taking some trouble in the matter. But if it is impossible for him to acquire the pronunciation, it would be better to mispronounce Chaucer's lines than to leave them unread.

In reading the story two points should be constantly kept in mind, namely, a thorough comprehension of the story and a definite study of the style. If the pupil comprehends the story perfectly he will be able at any point to give in his own words the argument, the description, or the senti-ments, as well as the events. In studying the style he will need somewhat heroic treatment if he is to be saved from glittering generalities. It is hoped that the treatment given above of the style of Dryden will be a help toward definiteness.

The study of words and sentences may well be made the subject of written exercises, varied from day to day—one day a list of words used in their literal meanings, another day a list of effective descriptive words and phrases, another several loose sentences rewritten in more closely welded form, or with Dryden's imperfect sequence of tense cor-rected, and still another, a passage rewritten in more simple wording than Dryden's. These exer-cises may be used to give point to the pupil's read-ing without taking much of his time or of the teacher's, and may give a good amount of technical drill. A moment's comment on such a set of exercises at the beginning of a recitation will often impress a class more than long discussions when the pupils have done no writing. The same method may be made to bring out the further characteristics of Dryden's style. One passage may be rewritten —in prose, of course—to tell the story more com-pactly, another to omit Dryden's general or cynical comments, his lapses in unity, etc. Such paraphrasing with a definite purpose is invaluable, and will lead the pupil to make for himself discoveries about his author's characteristics, whereas paraphrasing with no other purpose than retelling the story is deadening.

The study of figures is not so important as that of words and sentences, but some treatment of them is advisable. The elementary grouping of figures into those that are founded on resemblance and those that are not, will clarify the subject in the pupil's mind. Personification is plentiful in the poem, and need not be dwelt upon; the similes speak for themselves; in the case of metaphors it is well to insist that the pupil fill out the comparison, even to the extent of making a complete simile. Metonymy, as the typical figure of the class not founded on resemblance, should be emphasized whenever the instance occurs, and carefully distinguished from metaphor.

The versification need not be dwelt on long. The pupil should however be able to scan the lines, and should learn to notice for himself poor rhymes, triple rhymes, the Alexandrine verses, and the mutilated rhythm of such lines as "The inevitable charms of Emily" (l. 232).

For any broad literary criticism the high school pupil is not ready. By attempting it he only befuddles himself, and takes away the pleasure of trained discrimination which awaits him in his college course if he confines himself to the a b c's of criticism before entering. The teacher, however, may read as broadly as he will and is the proper medium for whatever light is to be shed on the reading by the great critics.

The best aid to the pupil's imagination, as well as to his sense of style, is constant writing. The subjects of the themes written outside of class should come from the book in hand, but should be narrowly limited. The pupil will never know whether he has a definite idea in his own mind of the temple of Mars until he writes out the description of it from memory, nor will he ever be so well prepared to decide whether Dryden's description is vivid or not until he has made the attempt to describe the same thing himself. A half dozen short themes, for instance, one to describe Emily, one to tell what the pupil imagines Palamon and Arcite had done before the expedition against Thebes, one to tell what Theseus thought when he discovered them fighting, one on the lists—including a map of the place—one on one of the temples, and another on the funeral of Arcite, would be infinitely better than a long theme on a general subject.

The notes are not intended to supersede the dictionary. The meaning of even unusual words is not given if the words are defined in the standard dictionaries. A glossary of proper names is added for the benefit of pupils who have not a classical dictionary at hand, rather than for those who have. The footnotes are given in place of notes in passages where Chaucer's text explains Dryden's. In three instances long extracts from Chaucer's text have been given, in order that the pupil may make for himself a comparative study of the two styles. The teacher will find it an invaluable exercise for the pupil to compare the two texts, line for line, and to draw his own conclusions from his observations as definitely as though he were performing an experiment in chemistry. It is only from such clearly-defined training that a quickened literary sense will come to the mind of the average high school student. Meantime the teacher must foster the pupil's sense of beauty by keeping the main points of the story in mind, and by calling attention to well-chosen words, to well-turned phrases, and to well-conceived pictures.

BIBLIOGRAPHY

CHAUCER

Chaucer, English Men of Letters Series, Ward.
Studies in Chaucer, Lounsbury. Vol. III, Chap. II.
History of English Literature, Taine. Vol. I.
My Study Windows, Lowell.

TEXT OF CHAUCER.—An excellent and inexpensive edition of Chaucer is Morris and Skeat's *Prologue* and *Knightes Tale* in the Clarendon Press Series.

DRYDEN

Lives of the Poets, Johnson, edited by Matthew Arnold. Vol. II.
Dryden, Scott's Edition. Vol. I.
English Poets, Chalmers. Vol. VIII.
Dryden, English Men of Letters Series, Saintsbury.
History of English Literature, Taine. Vol. III.
Among My Books, Lowell.
Home Pictures of English Poets, Kate Sanborn.
Essay on Dryden, Macaulay.
The Age of Dryden, Richard Garnett.
Literary Essays, III, Lowell.

HER GRACE THE DUCHESS OF ORMOND,

WITH THE FOLLOWING POEM OF

PALAMON AND ARCITE, FROM CHAUCER.

MADAM,

The bard who first adorned our native tongue,
Tuned to his British lyre this ancient song;
Which Homer might without a blush rehearse,
And leaves a doubtful palm in Virgil's verse:
5 He matched their beauties, where they most excel;
Of love sung better, and of arms as well.

Vouchsafe, illustrious Ormond, to behold
What power the charms of beauty had of old;
Nor wonder if such deeds of arms were done,
10 Inspired by two fair eyes that sparkled like your
own.

If Chaucer by the best idea wrought,
And poets can divine each other's thought,
The fairest nymph before his eyes he set;
And then the fairest was Plantagenet,
15 Who three contending princes made her prize,
And ruled the rival nations with her eyes;
Who left immortal trophies of her fame,
And to the noblest order gave the name.

Like her, of equal kindred to the throne,
You keep her conquests, and extend your own :   20
As when the stars, in their ethereal race,
At length have rolled around the liquid space,
At certain periods they resume their place,
From   the   same   point of heaven   their   course
    advance,
And move in measures of their former dance ;   25
Thus, after length of ages, she returns,
Restored in you, and the same place adorns ;
Or you perform her office in the sphere,
Born of her blood, and make a new Platonic year.
    O true Plantagenet, O race divine,   30
(For beauty still is fatal to the line,)
Had Chaucer lived that angel-face to view,
Sure he had drawn his Emily from you ;
Or had you lived to judge the doubtful right,
Your noble Palamon had been the knight ;   35
And conquering Theseus from his side had sent
Your generous lord, to guide the Theban govern-
    ment.
    Time shall accomplish that ; and I shall see
A Palamon in him, in you an Emily.
    Already have the Fates your path prepared,   40
And sure presage your future sway declared :
When westward, like the sun, you took your way,
And from benighted Britain bore the day,
Blue Triton gave the signal from the shore,
The ready Nereids heard, and swam before   45
To smooth the seas ; a soft Etesian gale

But just inspired, and gently swelled the sail;
Portunus took his turn, whose ample hand
Heaved up the lightened keel and sunk the sand,
50 And steered the sacred vessel safe to land.
The land, if not restrained, had met your way,
Projected out a neck, and jutted to the sea.
Hibernia, prostrate at your feet, adored
In you the pledge of her expected lord,
55 Due to her isle; a venerable name;
His father and his grandsire known to fame;
Awed by that house, accustomed to command,
The sturdy kerns in due subjection stand,
Nor hear the reins in any foreign hand.
60 At your approach, they crowded to the port;
And scarcely landed, you create a court:
As Ormond's harbinger, to you they run,
For Venus is the promise of the Sun.
  The waste of civil wars, their towns destroyed,
65 Pales unhonoured, Ceres unemployed,
Were all forgot; and one triumphant day
Wiped all the tears of three campaigns away.
Blood, rapines, massacres, were cheaply bought,
So mighty recompense your beauty brought.
70 As when the dove returning bore the mark
Of earth restored to the long-labouring ark,
The relics of mankind, secure of rest,
Oped every window to receive the guest,
And the fair bearer of the message blessed;
75 So, when you came, with loud repeated cries,
The nation took an omen from your eyes,

And God advanced his rainbow in the skies,
To sign inviolable peace restored;
The saints, with solemn shouts, proclaimed the new
    accord.
When at your second coming you appear   80
(For I foretell that millenary year)
The sharpened share shall vex the soil no more,
But earth unbidden shall produce her store;
The land shall laugh, the circling ocean smile,
And Heaven's indulgence bless the holy isle.   85
Heaven from all ages has reserved for you
That happy clime, which venom never knew;
Or if it had been there, your eyes alone
Have power to chase all poison, but their own.
Now in this interval, which Fate has cast   90
Betwixt your future glories and your past,
This pause of power, 'tis Ireland's hour to mourn;
While England celebrates your safe return,
By which you seem the seasons to command,
And bring our summers back to their forsaken 95
    land.
The vanquished isle our leisure must attend,
Till the fair blessing we vouchsafe to send;
Nor can we spare you long, though often we may
    lend.
The dove was twice employed abroad, before
The world was dried and she returned no more.   100
Nor dare we trust so soft a messenger,
New from her sickness, to that northern air;
Rest here awhile your lustre to restore,

That they may see you as you shone before;
105 For yet, the eclipse not wholly past, you wade
Through some remains and dimness of a shade.

A subject in his prince may claim a right,
Nor suffer him with strength impaired to fight;
Till force returns, his ardour we restrain,
110 And curb his warlike wish to cross the main.

Now past the danger, let the learned begin
The inquiry, where disease could enter in;
How those malignant atoms forced their way,
What in the faultless frame they found to make
    their prey,
115 Where every element was weighed so well,
That Heaven alone, who mixed the mass, could tell
Which of the four ingredients could rebel;
And where, imprisoned in so sweet a cage,
A soul might well be pleased to pass an age.

120   And yet the fine materials made it weak;
Porcelain, by being pure, is apt to break.
Even to your breast the sickness durst aspire;
And, forced from that fair temple to retire,
Profanely set the holy place on fire.

125 In vain your lord, like young Vespasian, mourned,
When the fierce flames the sanctuary burned;
And I prepared to pay in verses rude
A most detested act of gratitude:
Even this had been your Elegy, which now
130 Is offered for your health, the table of my vow.

Your angel sure our Morley's mind inspired,
To find the remedy your ill required.

As once the Macedon, by Jove's decree,
Was taught to dream a herb for Ptolemy:
Or Heaven, which had such over-cost bestowed   135
As scarce it could afford to flesh and blood,
So liked the frame, he would not work anew,
To save the charges of another you;
Or by his middle science did he steer,
And saw some great contingent good appear,   140
Well worth a miracle to keep you here;
And for that end, preserved the precious mould,
Which all the future Ormonds was to hold;
And meditated, in his better mind,
An heir from you, who may redeem the failing 145
    kind.

  Blessed be the power which has at once restored
The hopes of lost succession to your lord;
Joy to the first and last of each degree,
Virtue to courts, and, what I longed to see,
To you the Graces, and the Muse to me.   150

  O daughter of the Rose! whose cheeks unite
The differing titles of the Red and White;
Who Heaven's alternate beauty well display,
The blush of morning, and the milky way;
Whose face is Paradise, but fenced from sin;   155
For God in either eye has placed a cherubin.

  All is your lord's alone; even absent, he
Employs the care of chaste Penelope.
For him you waste in tears your widowed hours,
For him your curious needle paints the flowers;   160
Such works of old imperial dames were taught,

Such for Ascanius, fair Elisa wrought.
   The soft recesses of your hours improve
The three fair pledges of your happy love;
165 All other parts of pious duty done,
You owe your Ormond nothing but a son,
To fill in future times his father's place,
And wear the garter of his mother's race.

PALAMON AND ARCITE

OR, THE KNIGHT'S TALE

BOOK I

In days of old there lived, of mighty fame,
A valiant Prince, and Theseus was his name;
A chief, who more in feats of arms excelled,
The rising nor the setting sun beheld.
5 Of Athens he was lord; much land he won,
And added foreign countries to his crown.
In Scythia with the warrior Queen he strove,
Whom first by force he conquered, then by love;
He brought in triumph back the beauteous dame,
10 With whom her sister, fair Emilia, came.
With honour to his home let Theseus ride,
With Love to friend, and Fortune for his guide,
And his victorious army at his side.
I pass their warlike pomp, their proud array,
15 Their shouts, their songs, their welcome on the
      way;
  But, were it not too long, I would recite
The feats of Amazons, the fatal fight

5.—Compare Chaucer's opening lines:

    Whylom, as olde stories tellen us,
    Ther was a duk that highte Theseus;
    Of Athenes he was lord and governour,
    And in his tyme swich a conquerour
    That gretter was ther noon under the sonne.
    Ful many a riche contree hadde he wonne.

Betwixt the hardy Queen and hero Knight;
The town besieged, and how much blood it cost
The female army, and the Athenian host;   20
The spousals of Hippolyta the Queen;
What tilts and turneys at the feast were seen;
The storm at their return, the ladies' fear:
But these, and other things, I must forbear.
The field is spacious I design to sow,   25
With oxen far unfit to draw the plough:
The remnant of my tale is of a length
To tire your patience, and to waste my strength;
And trivial accidents shall be forborn,
That others may have time to take their turn,   30
As was at first enjoined us by mine host,
That he, whose tale is best and pleases most,
Should win his supper at our common cost.

And therefore where I left, I will pursue
This ancient story, whether false or true,   35
In hope it may be mended with a new.
The Prince I mentioned, full of high renown,
In this array drew near the Athenian town;
When, in his pomp and utmost of his pride
Marching, he chanced to cast his eye aside,   40
And saw a quire of mourning dames, who lay

---

33 (33)[1].—And lat see now who shal the soper winne,

41 (39).—Wher that ther kneled in the hye weye
       A compaignye of ladies, tweye and tweye,
       Ech after other, clad in clothes blake,

---

[1] The first numbers are those of Dryden's lines, the second those of Chaucer's (Clarendon Press edition).

By two and two across the common way:
At his approach they raised a rueful cry,
And beat their breasts, and held their hands on high,
45 Creeping and crying, till they seized at last
His courser's bridle and his feet embraced.
   "Tell me," said Theseus, "what and whence
     you are,
And why this funeral pageant you prepare?
Is this the welcome of my worthy deeds,
50 To meet my triumph in ill-omened weeds?
Or envy you my praise, and would destroy
With grief my pleasures, and pollute my joy?
Or are you injured, and demand relief?
Name your request, and I will ease your grief."
55   The most in years of all the mourning train
Began; but swounded first away for pain;
Then scarce recovered spoke: "Nor envy we
Thy great renown, nor grudge thy victory;
'Tis thine, O King, the afflicted to redress,
60 And fame has filled the world with thy success:
We wretched women sue for that alone,
Which of thy goodness is refused to none;
Let fall some drops of pity on our grief,
If what we beg be just, and we deserve relief;
65 For none of us, who now thy grace implore,
But held the rank of sovereign queen before;
Till thanks to giddy Chance, which never bears
That mortal bliss should last for length of years,

---

55 (54).—The eldest lady of hem alle spak,
67 (67).—Thanked be Fortune, and hir false wheel.

She cast us headlong from our high estate,
And here in hope of thy return we wait,   70
And long have waited in the temple nigh,
Built to the gracious goddess Clemency.
But reverence thou the power whose name it bears,
Relieve the oppressed, and wipe the widow's tears.
I, wretched I, have other fortune seen,   75
The wife of Capaneus, and once a Queen:
At Thebes he fell; cursed be the fatal day!
And all the rest thou seest in this array
To make their moan, their lords in battle lost
Before that town besieged by our confederate host.   80
But Creon, old and impious, who commands
The Theban city, and usurps the lands,
Denies the rites of funeral fires to those
Whose breathless bodies yet he calls his foes.
Unburned, unburied, on a heap they lie;   85
Such is their fate, and such his tyranny;
No friend has leave to bear away the dead,
But with their lifeless limbs his hounds are fed."
At this she shrieked aloud; the mournful train
Echoed her grief, and, grovelling on the plain,   90

---

81 (82).—Fulfild of ire and of iniquitee.
89 (91).—
    They fillen gruf,[1] and cryden pitously,
    'Have on us wrecched wommen som mercy,
    And lat our sorwe sinken in thyn herte.'
Notice that it is Dryden's straining after dramatic
effect here that blinds him to the real feeling of the
scene.

---

[1] Fell on their faces.

With groans, and hands upheld, to move his mind,
Besought his pity to their helpless kind.
　　The Prince was touched, his tears began to flow,
And as his tender heart would break in two,
95 He sighed; and could not but their fate deplore,
So wretched now, so fortunate before.
Then lightly from his lofty steed he flew,
And raising one by one the suppliant crew,
To comfort each, full solemnly he swore,
100 That by the faith which knights to knighthood bore,
And whate'er else to chivalry belongs,
He would not cease, till he revenged their wrongs:
That Greece should see performed what he declared,
And cruel Creon find his just reward.
105 He said no more, but shunning all delay,
Rode on, nor entered Athens on his way:
But left his sister and his queen behind,
And waved his royal banner in the wind,
Where in an argent field the God of War
110 Was drawn triumphant on his iron car;
Red was his sword, and shield, and whole attire,
And all the godhead seemed to glow with fire;
Even the ground glittered where the standard flew,
And the green grass was dyed to sanguine hue.
115 High on his pointed lance his pennon bore
His Cretan fight, the conquered Minotaur:
The soldiers shout around with generous rage,
And in that victcry their own presage.

---

100 (101).—And swoor his oth, as he was trewe knight,
105 (116).—And forth he rit; ther is namore to telle.

He praised their ardour, inly pleased to see
His host, the flower of Grecian chivalry.   120
All day he marched, and all the ensuing night,
And saw the city with returning light.
The process of the war I need not tell,
How Theseus conquered, and how Creon fell;
Or after, how by storm the walls were won,   125
Or how the victor sacked and burned the town;
How to the ladies he restored again
The bodies of their lords in battle slain;
And with what ancient rites they were interred;
All these to fitter times shall be deferred: 130
I spare the widows' tears, their woful cries,
And howling at their husbands' obsequies;
How Theseus at these funerals did assist,
And with what gifts the mourning dames dismissed.

Thus when the victor chief had Creon slain,   135
And conquered Thebes, he pitched upon the plain
His mighty camp, and when the day returned,
The country wasted and the hamlets burned,
And left the pillagers, to rapine bred,
Without control to strip and spoil the dead.   140
There, in a heap of slain, among the rest
Two youthful knights they found beneath a load
    oppressed
Of slaughtered foes, whom first to death they sent,
The trophies of their strength, a bloody monument.

---

138 (146).—And dide with al the contree as him leste.[1]

---

[1] Listed, pleased.

¹⁴⁵ Both fair, and both of royal blood they seemed,
Whom kinsmen to the crown the heralds deemed;
That day in equal arms they fought for fame;
Their swords, their shields, their surcoats were the
 same.
Close by each other laid they pressed the ground,
¹⁵⁰ Their manly bosoms pierced with many a grisly
 wound;
Nor well alive nor wholly dead they were,
But some faint signs of feeble life appear;
The wandering breath was on the wing to part,
Weak was the pulse, and hardly heaved the
 heart.
¹⁵⁵ These two were sisters' sons; and Arcite one
Much famed in fields, with valiant Palamon.
From these their costly arms the spoilers rent,
And softly both conveyed to Theseus' tent;
Whom, known of Creon's line, and cured with
 care,
¹⁶⁰ He to his city sent as prisoners of the war;
Hopeless of ransom, and condemned to lie
In durance, doomed a lingering death to die.
 This done, he marched away with warlike
 sound,
And to his Athens turned with laurels crowned,
¹⁶⁵ Where happy long he lived, much loved, and more
 renowned.
But in a tower, and never to be loosed,

---

155 (155).—Of whiche two Arcita hight that oon,
 And that other knight hight Palamon.

The woful captive kinsmen are enclosed.

Thus year by year they pass, and day by day,
Till once, ('twas on the morn of cheerful May)
The young Emilia, fairer to be seen   170
Than the fair lily on the flowery green,
More fresh than May herself in blossoms new,
(For with the rosy colour strove her hue,)
Waked, as her custom was, before the day,
To do the observance due to sprightly May;   175

168-200 (175-197). — Compare Dryden's thirty-three
lines with Chaucer's twenty-three, noting what Dryden
adds and what he leaves out.

> This passeth yeer by yeer, and day by day,
> Til it fil ones, in a morwe of May,
> That Emelye, that fairer was to sene
> Than is the lilie upon his stalke grene,
> And fressher than the May with floures newe—
> For with the rose colour strof hir hewe,
> I noot[1] which was the fairer of hem two—
> Er it were day, as was hir wone[2] to do,
> She was arisen, and al redy dight;[3]
> For May wol have no slogardye anight.
> The sesoun priketh every gentil herte,
> And maketh him out of his sleep to sterte,
> And seith, 'Arys, and do thyn observaunce.'
> This maked Emelye have remembraunce
> To doon honour to May, and for to ryse.
> Y-clothed was she fresh, for to devyse;[4]
> Hir yelow heer was broyded in a tresse,
> Bihynde hir bak, a yerde long, I gesse.
> And in the gardin, at the sonne up-riste,
> She walketh up and doun, and as hir liste[5]
> She gadereth floures, party[6] whyte and rede,
> To make a sotil[7] gerland for hir hede,
> And as an aungel hevenly she song.

---

[1] I know not.   [2] Wont, habit.   [3] Dressed.   [4] To tell or describe; the phrase is really superfluous.   [5] Listed, pleased.
[6] Partly.   [7] Subtle; the literal meaning is *finely woven*.

For sprightly May commands our youth to keep
The vigils of her night, and breaks their sluggard
    sleep;
Each gentle breast with kindly warmth she moves;
Inspires new flames, revives extinguished loves.
180 In this remembrance Emily ere day
Arose, and dressed herself in rich array,
Fresh as the month, and as the morning fair;
Adown her shoulders fell her length of hair:
A ribband did the braided tresses bind,
185 The rest was loose, and wantoned in the wind:
Aurora had but newly chased the night,
And purpled o'er the sky with blushing light,
When to the garden-walk she took her way,
To sport and trip along in cool of day,
190 And offer maiden vows in honour of the May.
    At every turn, she made a little stand,
And thrust among the thorns her lily hand
To draw the rose, and every rose she drew,
She shook the stalk, and brushed away the dew;
195 Then party-coloured flowers of white and red
She wove, to make a garland for her head:
This done, she sung and carolled out so clear,
That men and angels might rejoice to hear;
Even wondering Philomel forgot to sing,
200 And learned from her to welcome in the spring.
The tower, of which before was mention made,
Within whose keep the captive knights were laid,
Built of a large extent, and strong withal,
Was one partition of the palace wall;

The garden was enclosed within the square,   205
Where young Emilia took the morning air.
  It happened Palamon, the prisoner knight,
Restless for woe, arose before the light,
And with his jailer's leave desired to breathe
An air more wholesome than the damps beneath. 210
This granted, to the tower he took his way,
Cheered with the promise of a glorious day:
Then cast a languishing regard around,
And saw, with hateful eyes, the temples crowned
With golden spires, and all the hostile ground.   215
He sighed, and turned his eyes, because he knew
'Twas but a larger jail he had in view;
Then looked below, and from the castle's height
Beheld a nearer and more pleasing sight;
The garden, which before he had not seen   220
In spring's new livery clad of white and green,
Fresh flowers in wide parterres, and shady walks
        between.
This viewed, but not enjoyed, with arms across
He stood, reflecting on his country's loss;
Himself an object of the public scorn,   225
And often wished he never had been born.
At last, (for so his destiny required),
With walking giddy, and with thinking tired,
He through a little window cast his sight,
Though thick of bars, that gave a scanty light;   230
But even that glimmering served him to descry
The inevitable charms of Emily.
  Scarce had he seen, but seized with sudden smart,

Stung to the quick, he felt it at his heart;
235 Struck blind with overpowering light he stood,
Then started back amazed, and cried aloud.

    Young Arcite heard; and up he ran with haste,
To help his friend, and in his arms embraced;
And asked him why he looked so deadly wan,
240 And whence, and how, his change of cheer began?
Or who had done the offence? "But if," said he,
"Your grief alone is hard captivity,
For love of Heaven with patience undergo
A cureless ill, since Fate will have it so:
245 So stood our horoscope in chains to lie,
And Saturn in the dungeon of the sky,
Or other baleful aspect, ruled our birth
When all the friendly stars were under earth;
Whate'er betides, by Destiny 'tis done;
250 And better bear like men than vainly seek to shun."

    "Nor of my bonds," said Palamon again,
"Nor of unhappy planets I complain;
But when my mortal anguish caused my cry,
The moment I was hurt through either eye;
255 Pierced with a random shaft, I faint away,
And perish with insensible decay:
A glance of some new goddess gave the wound,
Whom, like Actæon, unaware I found.
Look how she walks along yon shady space;
260 Not Juno moves with more majestic grace,
And all the Cyprian queen is in her face.
If thou art Venus, (for thy charms confess
That face was formed in heaven), nor art thou less,

Disguised in habit, undisguised in shape,
O help us captives from our chains to scape!　265
But if our doom be past in bonds to lie
For life, and in a loathsome dungeon die,
Then be thy wrath appeased with our disgrace,
And show compassion to the Theban race,
Oppressed by tyrant power!''—While yet he spoke,　270
Arcite on Emily had fixed his look;
The fatal dart a ready passage found
And deep within his heart infixed the wound:
So that if Palamon were wounded sore
Arcite was hurt as much as he or more.　275
Then from his inmost soul he sighed, and said,
''The beauty I behold has struck me dead:
Unknowingly she strikes, and kills by chance;
Poison is in her eyes, and death in every glance.
Oh, I must ask; nor ask alone, but move　280
Her mind to mercy, or must die for love.''
　　Thus Arcite: and thus Palamon replies,
(Eager his tone, and ardent were his eyes,)
''Speakst thou in earnest, or in jesting vein?''
''Jesting,'' said Arcite, ''suits but ill with pain.''　285
''It suits far worse,'' (said Palamon again,
And bent his brows), ''with men who honour weigh,
Their faith to break, their friendship to betray;
But worst with thee, of noble lineage born,
My kinsman, and in arms my brother sworn.　290
Have we not plighted each our holy oath,

---

266 (250).—And if so be my destinee be shapen
　　　　By eterne word to dyen in prisoun,

That one should be the common good of both;
One soul should both inspire, and neither prove
His fellow's hindrance in pursuit of love?
295 To this before the Gods we gave our hands,
And nothing but our death can break the bands.
This binds thee, then, to farther my design,
As I am bound by vow to farther thine:
Nor canst, nor darest thou, traitor, on the plain
300 Appeach my honour, or thy own maintain,
Since thou art of my council, and the friend
Whose faith I trust, and on whose care depend.
And wouldst thou court my lady's love, which I
Much rather than release, would choose to die?
305 But thou, false Arcite, never shalt obtain
Thy bad pretence: I told thee first my pain:
For first my love began ere thine was born;
Thou as my council, and my brother sworn,
Art bound to assist my eldership of right,
310 Or justly to be deemed a perjured knight.''
    Thus Palamon: but Arcite with disdain
In haughty language thus replied again:
''Forsworn thyself: the traitor's odious name
I first return, and then disprove thy claim.
315 If love be passion, and that passion nurst
With strong desires, I loved the lady first.
Canst thou pretend desire, whom zeal inflamed
To worship, and a power celestial named?

---

313 (295).—

    'Thou shalt,' quod he, 'be rather fals than I;
    But thou art fals, I telle thee utterly.'

Thine was devotion to the blest above,
I saw the woman, and desired her love;   320
First owned my passion, and to thee commend
The important secret, as my chosen friend.
Suppose (which yet I grant not) thy desire
A moment elder than my rival fire;
Can chance of seeing first thy title prove?   325
And knowst thou not, no law is made for love;
Law is to things which to free choice relate;
Love is not in our choice, but in our fate;
Laws are not positive; love's power we see
Is Nature's sanction, and her first decree.   330
Each day we break the bond of human laws
For love, and vindicate the common cause.
Laws for defence of civil rights are placed,
Love throws the fences down, and makes a general
    waste.
Maids, widows, wives without distinction fall;   335
The sweeping deluge, love, comes on, and covers
    all.
If then the laws of friendship I transgress,
I keep the greater, while I break the less;
And both are mad alike, since neither can possess.
Both hopeless to be ransomed, never more   340
To see the sun, but as he passes o'er.
Like Æsop's hounds contending for the bone,
Each pleaded right, and would be lord alone:
The fruitless fight continued all the day,

---

328 (311).—A man moot needes love, maugree his
heed. (A man must needs love in spite of reason.)

345 A cur came by, and snatched the prize away.
As courtiers therefore justle for a grant,
And when they break their friendship, plead their
    want,
So thou, if Fortune will thy suit advance,
Love on, nor envy me my equal chance:
350 For I must love, and am resolved to try
My fate, or failing in the adventure die.''
    Great was their strife, which hourly was renewed,
Till each with mortal hate his rival viewed:
Now friends no more, nor walking hand in hand;
355 But when they met, they made a surly stand,
And glared like angry lions as they passed,
And wished that every look might be their last.
    It chanced at length, Pirithous came to attend
This worthy Theseus, his familiar friend;
360 Their love in early infancy began,
And rose as childhood ripened into man,
Companions of the war; and loved so well,
That when one died, as ancient stories tell,
His fellow to redeem him went to hell.
365   But, to pursue my tale: to welcome home
His warlike brother is Pirithous come:
Arcite of Thebes was known in arms long since
And honoured by this young Thessalian prince.

---

349 (325).—Love if thee list; for I love and ay shal;
        And sothly,[1] leve[2] brother, this is al.

359 (333).—A worthy duk that highte Perotheus,
367 (344).—Duk Perotheus loved wel Arcite,

---

[1]Truly.   [2]Loved, beloved.

Theseus, to gratify his friend and guest,
Who made our Arcite's freedom his request,   370
Restored to liberty the captive knight;
But on these hard conditions I recite;
That if hereafter Arcite should be found
Within the compass of Athenian ground,
By day or night or on whate'er pretence,   375
His head should pay the forfeit of the offence.
To this Pirithous for his friend agreed,
And on his promise was the prisoner freed.
    Unpleased and pensive hence he takes his
      way,
At his own peril; for his life must pay.   380
Who now but Arcite mourns his bitter fate,
Finds his dear purchase, and repents too late?
"What have I gained," he said, "in prison
    pent,
If I but change my bonds for banishment?
And banished from her sight, I suffer more   385
In freedom, than I felt in bonds before;
Forced from her presence, and condemned to
    live,
Unwelcome freedom, and unthanked reprieve:
Heaven is not, but where Emily abides,
And where she's absent, all is hell besides.   390
Next to my day of birth, was that accurst,
Which bound my friendship to Pirithous first:
Had I not known that prince, I still had been
In bondage, and had still Emilia seen:
For though I never can her grace deserve,   395

'Tis recompense enough to see and serve.
O Palamon, my kinsman and my friend,
How much more happy fates thy love attend!
Thine is the adventure, thine the victory,
400 Well has thy fortune turned the dice for thee:
Thou on that angel's face mayest feed thy eyes,
In prison, no; but blissful paradise!
Thou daily seest that sun of beauty shine,
And lovest at least in love's extremest line.
405 I mourn in absence, love's eternal night;
And who can tell but since thou hast her sight,
And art a comely, young, and valiant knight,
Fortune (a various power) may cease to frown,
And by some ways unknown thy wishes crown?
4:0 But I, the most forlorn of human kind,
Nor help can hope, nor remedy can find;
But doomed to drag my loathsome life in care,
For my reward, must end it in despair.
Fire, water, air, and earth, and force of fates
415 That governs all, and Heaven that all creates,
Nor art, nor Nature's hand can ease my grief;
Nothing but death, the wretch's last relief:
Then farewell youth, and all the joys that dwell

---

396 (373).—

> Only the sighte of hir, whom that I serve,
> Though that I nevere hir grace may deserve,
> Wolde han suffised right ynough for me.

418 (391).—

> Wel oughte I sterve in wanhope[1] and distresse;
> Farwel my lyf, my lust,[2] and my gladnesse.

---

[1]Despair.   [2]Pleasure.

With youth and life, and life itself, farewell!

"But why, alas! do mortal men in vain   420
Of Fortune, Fate, or Providence complain?
God gives us what He knows our wants require,
And better things than those which we desire:
Some pray for riches; riches they obtain;
But, watched by robbers, for their wealth are slain: 425
Some pray from prison to be freed; and come,
When guilty of their vows, to fall at home;
Murdered by those they trusted with their life,
A favoured servant or a bosom wife.
Such dear-bought blessings happen every day,   430
Because we know not for what things to pray.
Like drunken sots about the streets we roam:
Well knows the sot he has a certain home,
Yet knows not how to find the uncertain place,
And blunders on, and staggers every pace.   435
Thus all seek happiness; but few can find,
For far the greater part of men are blind.
This is my case, who thought our utmost good
Was in one word of freedom understood:
The fatal blessing came: from prison free,   440
I starve abroad, and lose the sight of Emily."

Thus Arcite: but if Arcite thus deplore
His sufferings, Palamon yet suffers more.

---

432 (403).—We faren as he that dronke is as a mous;[1]

441 (415).—Sin that I may nat seen yow, Emelye,
            I nam but deed; ther nis[2] no remedye.

---

[1]Mouse. "As drunk as a mouse" and "as drunk as a rat" are
old sayings.   [2]Is not. The double negative is common in Chaucer.

For when he knew his rival freed and gone,
445 He swells with wrath; he makes outrageous moan;
He frets, he fumes, he stares, he stamps the
    ground;
The hollow tower with clamours rings around:
With briny tears he bathed his fettered feet,
And dropped all o'er with agony of sweat.
450 "Alas!" he cried, "I, wretch, in prison pine,
Too happy rival, while the fruit is thine:
Thou livest at large, thou drawest thy native air,
Pleased with thy freedom, proud of my despair:
Thou mayest, since thou hast youth and courage
    joined,
455 A sweet behaviour and a solid mind,
Assemble ours, and all the Theban race,
To vindicate on Athens thy disgrace;
And after (by some treaty made), possess
Fair Emily, the pledge of lasting peace.
460 So thine shall be the beauteous prize, while I
Must languish in despair, in prison die.
Thus all the advantage of the strife is thine,
Thy portion double joys, and double sorrows mine."
The rage of jealousy then fired his soul,
465 And his face kindled like a burning coal:
Now cold despair, succeeding in her stead,
To livid paleness turns the glowing red.
His blood, scarce liquid, creeps within his veins,

---

460 (435).—
                                 Greet is thin avauntage,
More than is myn, that sterve here in a cage.

Like water which the freezing wind constrains.
Then thus he said: "Eternal Deities,   470
Who rule the world with absolute decrees,
And write whatever time shall bring to pass,
With pens of adamant on plates of brass;
What is the race of human kind your care
Beyond what all his fellow-creatures are?   475
He with the rest is liable to pain,
And like the sheep, his brother-beast, is slain.
Cold, hunger, prisons, ills without a cure,
All these he must, and guiltless oft, endure;
Or does your justice, power, or prescience fail,   480
When the good suffer and the bad prevail?
What worse to wretched virtue could befal,
If Fate or giddy Fortune governed all?
Nay, worse than other beasts is our estate:
Them, to pursue their pleasures, you create;   485
We, bound by harder laws, must curb our will,
And your commands, not our desires, fulfil;
Then, when the creature is unjustly slain,
Yet, after death at least, he feels no pain;
But man in life surcharged with woe before,   490
Not freed when dead, is doomed to suffer more.
A serpent shoots his sting at unaware;
An ambushed thief forelays a traveller;
The man lies murdered, while the thief and
    snake,
One gains the thickets, and one thrids the brake. 495

---

488 (461).—
    And whan a beest is deed, he hath no peyne;

·This let divines decide; but well I know,
Just or unjust, I have my share of woe;
Through Saturn seated in a luckless place,
And Juno's wrath, that persecutes my race;
500 Or Mars and Venus in a quartil move
My pangs of jealousy for Arcite's love."
    Let Palamon oppressed in bondage mourn,
While to his exiled rival we return.
By this the sun, declining from his height,
505 The day had shortened to prolong the night:
The lengthened night gave length of misery,
Both to the captive lover and the free:
For Palamon in endless prison mourns,
And Arcite forfeits life if he returns;
510 The banished never hopes his love to see,
Nor hopes the captive lord his liberty.
'Tis hard to say who suffers greater pains;
One sees his love, but cannot break his chains;
One free, and all his motions uncontrolled,
515 Beholds whate'er he would but what he would behold.
Judge as you please, for I will haste to tell
What fortune to the banished knight befel.
    When Arcite was to Thebes returned again,
The loss of her he loved renewed his pain;

---

496 (465).—
    The answere of this I lete[1] to divynis,
    But wel I woot,[2] that in this world gret pyne[3] is.

511 (489).—
    Yow loveres axe I now this questioun,
    Who hath the worse, Arcite or Palamoun?

---

[1]Leave.   [2]Know.   [3]Pain.

What could be worse than never more to see   520
His life, his soul, his charming Emily?
He raved with all the madness of despair,
He roared, he beat his breast, he tore his hair.
Dry sorrow in his stupid eyes appears,
For wanting nourishment, he wanted tears;   525
His eyeballs in their hollow sockets sink,
Bereft of sleep; he loathes his meat and drink;
He withers at his heart, and looks as wan
As the pale spectre of a murdered man:
That pale turns yellow, and his face receives   530
The faded hue of sapless boxen leaves;
In solitary groves he makes his moan,
Walks early out, and ever is alone;
Nor, mixed in mirth, in youthful pleasure shares,
But sighs when songs and instruments he hears.   535
His spirits are so low, his voice is drowned,
He hears as from afar, or in a swound,
Like the deaf murmurs of a distant sound:
Uncombed his locks and squalid his attire,
Unlike the trim of love and gay desire;   540
But full of museful mopings, which presage

---

527 (503).—
    His sleep, his mete, his drink is him biraft,[1]
    That lene he wex,[2] and drye as is a shaft.[3]

541 (519).—And shortly, turned was al up-so-doun
    Bothe habit and eek[4] disposicioun
    Of him, this woful lovere daun[5] Arcite.

---

[1]Bereft; the modern idiom is, he was bereft of sleep, etc.
[2]Grew. [3]Arrow or pole. Cf. the modern phrase "as dry as a stick." [4]Also. [5]A title of respect, originally given to mouks; it comes from *Dominus*. Chaucer himself was called Dan Chaucer.

The loss of reason and conclude in rage.

    This when he had endured a year and more,
Now wholly changed from what he was before,
545 It happened once, that, slumbering as he lay,
He dreamt (his dream began at break of day)
That Hermes o'er his head in air appeared,
And with soft words his drooping spirits cheered:
His hat adorned with wings disclosed the god,
550 And in his hand he bore the sleep-compelling rod:
Such as he seemed, when, at his sire's command,
On Argus' head he laid the snaky wand.
"Arise," he said, "to conquering Athens go;
There Fate appoints an end of all thy woe."
555 The fright awakened Arcite with a start,
Against his bosom bounced his heaving heart;
But soon he said, with scarce recovered breath,
"And thither will I go, to meet my death,
Sure to be slain; but death is my desire,
560 Since in Emilia's sight I shall expire."
By chance he spied a mirror while he spoke,
And gazing there beheld his altered look;

---

550 (529).—
    His slepy yerde[1] in hond he bar uprighte;
    An hat he werede[2] up-on his heres[3] brighte.

556 (535).—Chaucer says only:
    And with that word Arcite wook[4] and sterte.

559 (538).—Ne[5] for the drede of deeth shal I nat spare
    To see my lady, that I love and serve;
    In hir presence I recche[6] nat to sterve.[7]

---

[1]Wand.   [2]Wore.   [3]Hair, locks.   [4]Woke.   [5]Nor; a double
negative.   [6]Recche, make no account of (dying).   [7]Die.

Wondering, he saw his features and his hue
So much were changed, that scarce himself he
    knew.
A sudden thought then starting in his mind,   565
"Since I in Arcite cannot Arcite find,
The world may search in vain with all their eyes,
But never penetrate through this disguise.
Thanks to the change which grief and sickness
    give,
In low estate I may securely live,   570
And see, unknown, my mistress day by day."
He said, and clothed himself in coarse array,
A labouring hind in show; then forth he went,
And to the Athenian towers his journey bent:
One squire attended in the same disguise,   575
Made conscious of his master's enterprise.
Arrived at Athens, soon he came to court,
Unknown, unquestioned, in that thick resort:
Proffering for hire his service at the gate,
To drudge, draw water, and to run or wait.   580
    So fair befel him, that for little gain
He served at first Emilia's chamberlain;
And watchful all advantages to spy,
Was still at hand, and in his master's eye;
And as his bones were big, and sinews strong,   585
Refused no toil that could to slaves belong;
But from deep wells with engines water drew,
And used his noble hands the wood to hew.
He passed a year at least attending thus
On Emily, and called Philostratus.   590

But never was there man of his degree
So much esteemed, so well beloved as he.
So gentle of condition was he known,
That through the court his courtesy was blown:
595 All think him worthy of a greater place,
And recommend him to the royal grace;
That exercised within a higher sphere,
His virtues more conspicuous might appear.
Thus by the general voice was Arcite praised,
600 And by great Theseus to high favour raised;
Among his menial servants first enrolled,
And largely entertained with sums of gold:
Besides what secretly from Thebes was sent,
Of his own income, and his annual rent.
605 This well employed, he purchased friends and fame,
But cautiously concealed from whence it came.
Thus for three years he lived with large increase,
In arms of honour, and esteem in peace;
To Theseus' person he was ever near;
610 And Theseus for his virtues held him dear.

---

600 (582).—
　　　That of his chambre he made him a squyer,

BOOK II

While Arcite lives in bliss, the story turns
Where hopeless Palamon in prison mourns.
For six long years immured, the captive knight
Had dragged his chains, and scarcely seen the
    light:
Lost liberty and love at once he bore;   615
His prison pained him much, his passion more:
Nor dares he hope his fetters to remove,
Nor ever wishes to be free from love.

But when the sixth revolving year was run,
And May within the Twins received the sun,   620
Were it by Chance, or forceful Destiny,
Which forms in causes first whate'er shall be,
Assisted by a friend one moonless night,
This Palamon from prison took his flight:
A pleasant beverage he prepared before   625
Of wine and honey mixed, with added store
Of opium; to his keeper this he brought,
Who swallowed unaware the sleepy draught,

---

616 (598).—That wood[1] out of his wit he goth[2] for wo:

622 (608).—As, whan a thing is shapen,[3] it shal be,

623 (605).—The thridde[4] night, (as olde bokes seyn,
        That al this storie tellen more pleyn).

---

[1]Mad.   [2]Goeth.   [3]Destined.   [4]Third.

And snored secure till morn, his senses bound
630 In slumber, and in long oblivion drowned.
Short was the night, and careful Palamon
Sought the next covert ere the rising sun.
A thick-spread forest near the city lay,
To this with lengthened strides he took his way,
635 (For far he could not fly, and feared the day.)
Safe from pursuit, he meant to shun the light,
Till the brown shadows of the friendly night
To Thebes might favour his intended flight.
When to his country come, his next design
640 Was all the Theban race in arms to join,
And war on Theseus, till he lost his life,
Or won the beauteous Emily to wife.
Thus while his thoughts the lingering day beguile,
To gentle Arcite let us turn our style;
645 Who little dreamt how nigh he was to care,
Till treacherous fortune caught him in the snare.
The morning lark, the messenger of day,
Saluted in her song the morning gray;
And soon the sun arose with beams so bright,

---

629 (615). —
    That al that night, thogh that men wolde him shake
    The gayler[1] sleep, he mighte nat awake;

647 (633).—
    The bisy larke, messager of daye,
    Salueth in hir song the morwe graye;
    And fyry Phebus ryseth up so brighte,
    That al the orient laugheth of the lighte,
    And with his stremes dryeth in the greves[2]
    The silver dropes, hanging on the leves.

---

[1]Jailer.   [2]Groves.

That all the horizon laughed to see the joyous 650
    sight;
He with his tepid rays the rose renews,
And licks the dropping leaves, and dries the dews;
When Arcite left his bed, resolved to pay
Observance to the month of merry May,
Forth on his fiery steed betimes he rode, 655
That scarcely prints the turf on which he trod:
At ease he seemed, and prancing o'er the plains,
Turned only to the grove his horse's reins,
The grove I named before, and, lighting there,
A woodbind garland sought to crown his hair; 660
Then turned his face against the rising day,
And raised his voice to welcome in the May:
  "For thee, sweet month, the groves green
    liveries wear,
If not the first, the fairest of the year:
For thee the Graces lead the dancing hours, 665
And Nature's ready pencil paints the flowers:
When thy short reign is past, the feverish sun

---

657 (644).—
    He on a courser, sterting[1] as the fyr,[2]
    Is riden into the feeldes, him to pleye,
    Out of the court, were it a myle or tweye;

660 (650).—
    Were it of woodebynde or hawethorn-leves,
    And loude he song ageyn[3] the sonne shene.

662-672 (652).—Chaucer has only three lines:
    May, with alle thy floures and thy grene,
    Wel-come be thou, wel faire fresshe May,
    I hope that I som grene gete may.

---

[1]Leaping, prancing.   [2]Fire.   [3]Modern idiom, "in the sunshine."

The sultry tropic fears, and moves more slowly on.
So may thy tender blossoms fear no blight,
670 Nor goats with venomed teeth thy tendrils bite,
As thou shalt guide my wandering feet to find
The fragrant greens I seek, my brows to bind."
   His vows addressed, within the grove he strayed,
Till Fate or Fortune near the place conveyed
675 His steps where secret Palamon was laid.
Full little thought of him the gentle knight,
Who flying death had there concealed his flight,
In brakes and brambles hid, and shunning mortal
    sight;
And less he knew him for his hated foe,
680 But feared him as a man he did not know.
But as it has been said of ancient years,
That fields are full of eyes and woods have ears,
For this the wise are ever on their guard,
For unforeseen, they say, is unprepared.
685 Uncautious Arcite thought himself alone,
And less than all suspected Palamon,
Who, listening, heard him, while he searched the
    grove,
And loudly sung his roundelay of love:
But on the sudden stopped, and silent stood,

---

675 (658).—
    Ther as by aventure this Palamoun
    Was in a bush, that no man mighte him see,
    For sore afered of his deeth was he.

687 (669).—
    For in the bush he[1] sitteth now ful stille.

---
[1] Palamon.

(As lovers often muse, and change their mood;)   690
Now high as heaven, and then as low as hell,
Now up, now down, as buckets in a well:
For Venus, like her day, will change her cheer,
And seldom shall we see a Friday clear.
Thus Arcite, having sung, with altered hue   695
Sunk on the ground, and from his bosom drew
A desperate sigh, accusing Heaven and Fate,
And angry Juno's unrelenting hate:
"Cursed be the day when first I did appear;
Let it be blotted from the calendar,   700
Lest it pollute the month, and poison all the year.
Still will the jealous Queen pursue our race?
Cadmus is dead, the Theban city was:
Yet ceases not her hate; for all who come
From Cadmus are involved in Cadmus' doom.   705
I suffer for my blood: unjust decree,
That punishes another's crime on me.
In mean estate I serve my mortal foe,
The man who caused my country's overthrow.
This is not all; for Juno, to my shame,   710
Has forced me to forsake my former name;
Arcite I was, Philostratus I am.
That side of heaven is all my enemy:
Mars ruined Thebes; his mother ruined me.
Of all the royal race remains but one   715

---

712 (699).—
      But ther as I was wont to hote[1] Arcite,
      Now highte I Philostrate, noght worth a myte.

---

[1] Be called.

Besides myself, the unhappy Palamon,
Whom Theseus holds in bonds and will not free;
Without a crime, except his kin to me.
Yet these and all the rest I could endure;
720 But love's a malady without a cure:
Fierce Love has pierced me with his fiery dart,
He fries within, and hisses at my heart.
Your eyes, fair Emily, my fate pursue;
I suffer for the rest, I die for you.
725 Of such a goddess no time leaves record,
Who burned the temple where she was adored:
And let it burn, I never will complain,
Pleased with my sufferings, if you knew my pain.''
At this a sickly qualm his heart assailed,
730 His ears ring inward, and his senses failed.
No word missed Palamon of all he spoke;
But soon to deadly pale he changed his look;
He trembled every limb, and felt a smart,
As if cold steel had glided through his heart;
735 Nor longer stayed, but starting from his place,
Discovered stood, and showed his hostile face:
"False traitor, Arcite, traitor to thy blood,
Bound by thy sacred oath to seek my good,
Now art thou found forsworn for Emily,
740 And darest attempt her love, for whom I die.
So hast thou cheated Theseus with a wile,
Against thy vow, returning to beguile

---

735 (720).—
　　As he were wood, with face deed and pale,
　　He sterte him up out of the buskes thikke,

Under a borrowed name: as false to me,
So false thou art to him who set thee free.
But rest assured, that either thou shalt die,   745
Or else renounce thy claim in Emily;
For though unarmed I am, and, freed by chance,
Am here without my sword or pointed lance:
Hope not, base man, unquestioned hence to go,
For I am Palamon, thy mortal foe."   750
    Arcite, who heard his tale and knew the man,
His sword unsheathed, and fiercely thus began:
"Now, by the gods who govern heaven above,
Wert thou not weak with hunger, mad with love,
That word had been thy last; or in this grove   755
This hand should force thee to renounce thy love;
The surety which I gave thee I defy:
Fool, not to know that love endures no tie,
And Jove but laughs at lovers' perjury.
Know, I will serve the fair in thy despite;   760
But since thou art my kinsman and a knight,
Here, have my faith, to-morrow in this grove
Our arms shall plead the titles of our love:
And Heaven so help my right, as I alone
Will come, and keep the cause and quarrel both   765
        unknown,
With arms of proof both for myself and thee;
Choose thou the best, and leave the worst to me.
And, that at better ease thou mayest abide,
Bedding and clothes I will this night provide,
And needful sustenance, that thou mayest be   770
A conquest better won, and worthy me."

His promise Palamon accepts; but prayed,
To keep it better than the first he made.
Thus fair they parted till the morrow's dawn;
775 For each had laid his plighted faith to pawn.
Oh Love! thou sternly dost thy power maintain,
And wilt not bear a rival in thy reign!
Tyrants and thou all fellowship disdain.
This was in Arcite proved and Palamon:
780 Both in despair, yet each would love alone.
Arcite returned, and, as in honour tied,
His foe with bedding and with food supplied;
Then, ere the day, two suits of armour sought,
Which borne before him on his steed he brought:
785 Both were of shining steel, and wrought so pure
As might the strokes of two such arms endure.
Now, at the time, and in the appointed place,
The challenger and challenged, face to face,
Approach; each other from afar they knew,
790 And from afar their hatred changed their hue.
So stands the Thracian herdsman with his spear,
Full in the gap, and hopes the hunted bear,
And hears him rustling in the wood, and sees
His course at distance by the bending trees:
795 And thinks, Here comes my mortal enemy,
And either he must fall in fight, or I:
This while he thinks, he lifts aloft his dart;
A generous chillness seizes every part,

---

775 (764).—
   When ech of hem had leyd his feith to borwe.[1]

_____

[1] Given his faith as a pledge.

The veins pour back the blood, and fortify the
    heart.
   Thus pale they meet; their eyes with fury burn; 800
None greets, for none the greeting will return;
But in dumb surliness each armed with care
His foe professed, as brother of the war;
Then both, no moment lost, at once advance
Against each other, armed with sword and lance: 805
They lash, they foin, they pass, they strive to bore
Their corslets, and the thinnest parts explore.
Thus two long hours in equal arms they stood,
And wounded wound, till both were bathed in
    blood
And not a foot of ground had either got,   810
As if the world depended on the spot.
Fell Arcite like an angry tiger fared,
And like a lion Palamon appeared:
Or, as two boars whom love to battle draws,
With rising bristles and with frothy jaws,   815
Their adverse breasts with tusks oblique they
    wound,
With grunts and groans the forest rings around.
So fought the knights, and fighting must abide,
Till Fate an umpire sends their difference to decide.
The power that ministers to God's decrees,   820

---

809 (802).—Up to the ancle foghte they in hir blood.

812 (812).—For certeinly oure appetytes here,
        Be it of werre, or pees,[1] or hate, or love,
        Al is this reuled by the sighte[2] above.

---

[1] Peace.   [2] Providence.

And executes on earth what Heaven foresees,
Called Providence, or Chance, or Fatal sway,
Comes with resistless force, and finds or makes her
    way.
Nor kings, nor nations, nor united power
825 One moment can retard the appointed hour;
And some one day, some wondrous chance appears,
Which happened not in centuries of years:
For sure, whate'er we mortals hate or love
Or hope or fear depends on powers above:
830 They move our appetites to good or ill,
And by foresight necessitate the will.
In Theseus this appears, whose youthful joy
Was beasts of chase in forests to destroy;
This gentle knight, inspired by jolly May,
835 Forsook his easy couch at early day,
And to the woods and wilds pursued his way.
Beside him rode Hippolyta the queen,
And Emily attired in lively green,
With horns and hounds and all the tuneful
    cry,
840 To hunt a royal hart within the covert nigh:
And, as he followed Mars before, so now
He serves the goddess of the silver bow.
The way that Theseus took was to the wood,
Where the two knights in cruel battle stood:
845 The laund on which they fought, the appointed
    place
In which the uncoupled hounds began the chase.

---

840 (824).—For after Mars he serveth now Diane.

Thither forth-right he rode to rouse the prey,
That shaded by the fern in harbour lay;
And thence dislodged, was wont to leave the wood
For open fields, and cross the crystal flood.   850
Approached, and looking underneath the sun,
He saw proud Arcite and fierce Palamon,
In mortal battle doubling blow on blow;
Like lightning flamed their fauchions to and fro,
And shot a dreadful gleam; so strong they strook, 855
There seemed less force required to fell an oak.
He gazed with wonder on their equal might,
Looked eager on, but knew not either knight.
Resolved to learn, he spurred his fiery steed
With goring rowels to provoke his speed.   860
The minute ended that began the race,
So soon he was betwixt them on the place;
And with his sword unsheathed, on pain of life
Commands both combatants to cease their strife;
Then with imperious tone pursues his threat: 865
"What are you? why in arms together met?
How dares your pride presume against my laws,
As in a listed field to fight your cause,

---

849 (834).—
> For thider was the hert wont have his flight,
> And over a brook, and so forth in his weye.

861 (847).—
> And at a stert he was bitwix hem two,
> And pullede out a swerd and cryed, 'Ho!
> Namore, up peyne[1] of lesing[2] of your heed.'

---

[1] On pain.   [2] Losing.

Unasked the royal grant; no marshal by,
870 As knightly rites require, nor judge to try?"
Then Palamon, with scarce recovered breath,
Thus hasty spoke: "We both deserve the death,
And both would die; for look the world around,
A pair so wretched is not to be found.
875 Our life's a load; encumbered with the charge,
We long to set the imprisoned soul at large.
Now, as thou art a sovereign judge, decree
The rightful doom of death to him and me;
Let neither find thy grace, for grace is cruelty.
880 Me first, O, kill me first, and cure my woe;
Then sheath the sword of justice on my foe;
Or kill him first, for when his name is heard,
He foremost will receive his due reward.
Arcite of Thebes is he, thy mortal foe,
885 On whom thy grace did liberty bestow;
But first contracted, that, if ever found
By day or night upon the Athenian ground,
His head should pay the forfeit; see returned
The perjured knight, his oath and honour scorned:
890 For this is he, who, with a borrowed name
And proffered service, to thy palace came,
Now called Philostratus; retained by thee,
A traitor trusted, and in high degree,
Aspiring to the bed of beauteous Emily.
895 My part remains, from Thebes my birth I own,

---

880 (863).—But sle me first, for seynte[1] charitee;
      But sle my felawe eek as wel as me.

---

[1] Blessed.

And call myself the unhappy Palamon.
Think me not like that man; since no disgrace
Can force me to renounce the honour of my race.
Know me for what I am: I broke thy chain,
Nor promised I thy prisoner to remain: 900
The love of liberty with life is given,
And life itself the inferior gift of Heaven.
Thus without crime I fled; but farther know,
I, with this Arcite, am thy mortal foe:
Then give me death, since I thy life pursue;   905
For safeguard of thyself, death is my due.
More wouldst thou know?   I love bright Emily,
And for her sake and in her sight will die:
But kill my rival too, for he no less
Deserves; and I thy righteous doom will bless,   910
Assured that what I lose he never shall possess."
To this replied the stern Athenian Prince,
And sourly smiled: "In owning your offence
You judge yourself, and I but keep record
In place of law, while you pronounce the word.   915
Take your desert, the death you have decreed;
I seal your doom, and ratify the deed:
By Mars, the patron of my arms, you die."
     He said; dumb sorrow seized the standers-by.
The Queen, above the rest, by nature good,   920

---

909 (882).—But sle my felawe in the same wyse,
                   For bothe han we deserved to be slayn.
920 (890).—The quene anon, for verray wommanhede[1]
                   Gan for to wepe, and so dide Emelye,
                   And alle the ladies in the compaignye.

---

[1]Womanliness.

(The pattern formed of perfect womanhood)
For tender pity wept: when she began,
Through the bright quire the infectious virtue
    ran.
All dropt their tears, even the contended maid:
925 And thus among themselves they softly said:
"What eyes can suffer this unworthy sight!
Two youths of royal blood, renowned in fight,
The mastership of Heaven in face and mind,
And lovers, far beyond their faithless kind:
930 See their wide streaming wounds; they neither
    came
From pride of empire nor desire of fame:
Kings fight for kingdoms, madmen for applause;
But love for love alone, that crowns the lover's
    cause."
This thought, which ever bribes the beauteous kind,
935 Such pity wrought in every lady's mind,
They left their steeds, and prostrate on the place,
From the fierce King implored the offenders' grace.
    He paused a while, stood silent in his mood;
(For yet his rage was boiling in his blood:)
940 But soon his tender mind the impression felt.
(As softest metals are not slow to melt
And pity soonest runs in gentle minds:)
Then reasons with himself; and first he finds
His passion cast a mist before his sense,
945 And either made, or magnified the offence.
Offence! Of what? To whom? Who judged the
    cause?

The prisoner freed himself by Nature's laws;
Born free, he sought his right; the man he freed
Was perjured, but his love excused the deed:
Thus pondering, he looked under with his eyes,   950
And saw the women's tears, and heard their cries,
Which moved compassion more; he shook his head,
And softly sighing to himself he said:
  "Curse on the unpardoning prince, whom tears
    can draw
To no remorse, who rules by lion's law;   955
And deaf to prayers, by no submission bowed,
Rends all alike, the penitent and proud!"
At this with look serene he raised his head;
Reason resumed her place, and passion fled:
Then thus aloud he spoke:—"The power of Love,   960
In earth, and seas, and air, and heaven above,
Rules, unresisted, with an awful nod,
By daily miracles declared a god;
He blinds the wise, gives eye-sight to the blind;
And moulds and stamps anew the lover's mind.   965
Behold that Arcite, and this Palamon,
Freed from my fetters, and in safety gone,
What hindered either in their native soil

L. 953 (914).—
    And in his gentil herte he thoghte anoon,
    And softe un-to himself he seyde: 'Fy
    Up-on a lord that wol have no mercy,
    But been a leoun,[1] bothe in word and dede,'

960 (927).—The god of love, a! *benedicite,*
    How mighty and how greet a lord is he!

---

[1] Lion.

At ease to reap the harvest of their toil?
970 But Love, their lord, did otherwise ordain,
And brought them, in their own despite again,
To suffer death deserved; for well they know
'Tis in my power, and I their deadly foe.
The proverb holds, that to be wise and love,
975 Is hardly granted to the gods above.
See how the madmen bleed! Behold the gains
With which their master, Love, rewards their pains!
For seven long years, on duty every day,
Lo! their obedience, and their monarch's pay!
980 Yet, as in duty bound, they serve him on;
And ask the fools, they think it wisely done;
Nor ease nor wealth nor life itself regard,
For 'tis their maxim, love is love's reward.
This is not all; the fair, for whom they strove,
985 Nor knew before, nor could suspect their love,
Nor thought, when she beheld the fight from far,
Her beauty was the occasion of the war.
But sure a general doom on man is past,
And all are fools and lovers, first or last:
990 This both by others and myself I know,
For I have served their sovereign long ago;
Oft have been caught within the winding train
Of female snares, and felt the lover's pain,
And learned how far the. god can human hearts
    constrain.

---

974 (940).—Now loketh,[1] is nat that an heigh folye?
    Who may nat ben a fool, if that he love?

---

[1] Look.

To this remembrance, and the prayers of those   995
Who for the offending warriors interpose,
I give their forfeit lives, on this accord,
To do me homage as their sovereign lord;
And as my vassals, to their utmost might,
Assist my person and assert my right."   1000
This freely sworn, the knights their grace obtained;
Then thus the king his secret thought explained:
"If wealth or honour or a royal race,
Or each or all, may win a lady's grace,
Then either of you knights may well deserve   1005
A princess born; and such is she you serve:
For Emily is sister to the crown,
And but too well to both her beauty known:
But should you combat till you both were dead,
Two lovers cannot share a single bed.   1010
As, therefore, both are equal in degree,
The lot of both be left to destiny.
Now hear the award, and happy may it prove
To her, and him who best deserves her love.
Depart from hence in peace, and free as air,   1015
Search the wide world, and where you please
     repair;
But on the day when this returning sun
To the same point through every sign has run,
Then each of you his hundred knights shall bring,
In royal lists, to fight before the king;   1020
And then the knight, whom Fate or happy Chance
Shall with his friends to victory advance,
And grace his arms so far in equal fight,

From out the bars to force his opposite,
1025 Or kill, or make him recreant on the plain,
The prize of valour and of love shall gain;
The vanquished party shall their claim release,
And the long jars conclude in lasting peace.
The charge be mine to adorn the chosen
    ground,
1030 The theatre of war, for champions so renowned;
And take the patron's place of either knight,
With eyes impartial to behold the fight;
And Heaven of me so judge as I shall judge
    aright.
If both are satisfied with this accord,
1035 Swear by the laws of knighthood on my sword.''
    Who now but Palamon exults with joy?
And ravished Arcite seems to touch the sky.
The whole assembled troop was pleased as well,
Extolled the award, and on their knees they fell
1040 To bless the gracious King.   The knights, with
    leave
Departing from the place, his last commands
    receive;
On Emily with equal ardour look,
And from her eyes their inspiration took:
From thence to Thebes' old walls pursue their
    way,
1045 Each to provide his champions for the day.
    It might be deemed, on our historian's part,
Or too much negligence or want of art,
If he forgot the vast magnificence

Of royal Theseus, and his large expense.
He first enclosed for lists a level ground,   1050
The whole circumference a mile around;
The form was circular; and all without
A trench was sunk, to moat the place about.
Within, an amphitheatre appeared,
Raised in degrees, to sixty paces reared: 1055
That when a man was placed in one degree,
Height was allowed for him above to see.
   Eastward was built a gate of marble white;
The like adorned the western opposite.
A nobler object than this fabric was   1060
Rome never saw, nor of so vast a space:
For, rich with spoils of many a conquered land,
All arts and artists Theseus could command,
Who sold for hire, or wrought for better fame;
The master-painters and the carvers came.   1065
So rose within the compass of the year
An age's work, a glorious theatre.
Then o'er its eastern gate was raised above
A temple, sacred to the Queen of Love;
An altar stood below: on either hand   1070
A priest with roses crowned, who held a myrtle
    wand.

1049 (1027).—
    That swich a noble theatre as it was,
    I dar wel seyn that in this world ther nas.[1]

1056 (1033).—That whan a man was set on o[2] degree,
    He lette[3] nat his felawe for to see.

---

[1] Was not.   [2] One.   [3] Hindered.

The dome of Mars was on the gate opposed,
And on the north a turret was enclosed
Within the wall of alabaster white
1075 And crimson coral, for the Queen of Night,
Who takes in sylvan sports her chaste delight.
Within these oratories might you see
Rich carvings, portraitures, and imagery:
Where every figure to the life expressed
1080 The godhead's power to whom it was addressed.
In Venus' temple on the sides were seen
The broken slumbers of enamoured men;
Prayers that even spoke, and pity seemed to call,
And issuing sighs that smoked along the wall;
1085 Complaints and hot desires, the lover's hell,
And scalding tears that wore a channel where they
    fell;
And all around were nuptial bonds, the ties
Of love's assurance, and a train of lies,
That, made in lust, conclude in perjuries;
1090 Beauty, and Youth, and Wealth, and Luxury,
And sprightly Hope, and short-enduring Joy,
And Sorceries to raise the infernal powers,
And Sigils framed in planetary hours;
Expense, and After-thought, and idle Care,
1095 And Doubts of motley hue, and dark Despair;
Suspicions and fantastical Surmise,
And Jealousy suffused, with jaundice in her eyes,
Discolouring all she viewed, in tawny dressed,
Down-looked, and with a cuckow on her fist.
1100 Opposed to her, on the other side advance

The costly feast, the carol, and the dance,
Minstrels and music, poetry and play,
And balls by night, and turnaments by day.
All these were painted on the wall, and more;
With acts and monuments of times before;   1105
And others added by prophetic doom,
And lovers yet unborn, and loves to come:
For there the Idalian mount, and Citheron,
The court of Venus, was in colours drawn;
Before the palace gate, in careless dress   1110
And loose array, sat portress Idleness;
There by the fount Narcissus pined alone;
There Samson was; with wiser Solomon,
And all the mighty names by love undone.
Medea's charms were there, Circean feasts,   1115
With bowls that turned enamoured youths to beasts.
Here might be seen, that beauty, wealth, and wit,
And prowess to the power of love submit;
The spreading snare for all mankind is laid,
And lovers all betray, and are betrayed.   1120
The Goddess' self some noble hand had wrought;
Smiling she seemed, and full of pleasing thought,
From ocean as she first began to rise,
And smoothed the ruffled seas, and cleared the skies.

A lute she held; and on her head was seen

1119 (1093).—
    Lo, alle thise folk so caught were in hir las,[1]
    Til they for wo ful ofte seyde "allas."

---

[1] Net.

A wreath of roses red and myrtles green;
Her turtles fanned the buxom air above;
1130 And by his mother stood an infant Love,
With wings unfledged; his eyes were banded o'er,
His hands a bow, his back a quiver bore,
Supplied with arrows bright and keen, a deadly
   store.
But in the dome of mighty Mars the red
1135 With different figures all the sides were spread;
This temple, less in form, with equal grace,
Was imitative of the first in Thrace;
For that cold region was the loved abode
And sovereign mansion of the warrior god.
1140 The landscape was a forest wide and bare,
Where neither beast nor human kind repair,
The fowl that scent afar the borders fly,
And shun the bitter blast, and wheel about the sky.
A cake of scurf lies baking on the ground,
1145 And prickly stubs, instead of trees, are found;
Or woods with knots and knares deformed and old,
Headless the most, and hideous to behold.
A rattling tempest through the branches went,
That stripped them bare, and one sole way they bent.
1150 Heaven froze above severe, the clouds congeal,
And through the crystal vault appeared the stand-
   ing hail.
Such was the face without: a mountain stood
Threatening from high, and overlooked the wood:

1148 (1122).—
   As though a storm scholde bresten every bough:

Beneath the lowering brow, and on a bent,
The temple stood of Mars armipotent: 1155
The frame of burnished steel, that cast a glare
From far, and seemed to thaw the freezing air.
A straight long entry to the temple led,
Blind with high walls, and horror over head;
Thence issued such a blast, and hollow roar,   1160
As threatened from the hinge to heave the door;
In through that door a northern light there shone;
'Twas all it had, for windows there were none.
The gate was adamant; eternal frame,
Which, hewed by Mars himself, from Indian 1165
        quarries came,
The labour of a God; and all along
Tough iron plates were clenched to make it strong.
A tun about was every pillar there;
A polished mirror shone not half so clear.
There saw I how the secret felon wrought,   1170
And treason labouring in the traitor's thought.

There the red Anger dared the pallid Fear;
Next stood Hypocrisy, with holy leer,
Soft, smiling, and demurely looking down,   1175
But hid the dagger underneath the gown;
The assassinating wife, the household fiend;
And far the blackest there, the traitor-friend.
On the other side there stood Destruction bare,
Unpunished Rapine, and a waste of war;   1180

1174 (1141).—One line in Chaucer:
        The smyler with the knyf under the cloke.

Contest, with sharpened knives, in cloisters drawn,
And all with blood bespread the holy lawn.
Loud menaces were heard, and foul disgrace,
And brawling infamy, in language base;
1185 Till sense was lost in sound, and silence fled the
    place.
The slayer of himself yet saw I there,
The gore congealed was clottered in his hair;
With eyes half closed, and gaping mouth he lay,
And grim as when he breathed his sullen soul
    away.
1190 In midst of all the dome Misfortune sate,
And gloomy Discontent, and fell Debate,
And Madness laughing in his ireful mood;
And armed Complaint on theft; and cries of blood.
There was the murdered corps, in covert laid,
1195 And violent death in thousand shapes displayed:
The city to the soldier's rage resigned:
Successless wars, and poverty behind:
Ships burnt in fight, or forced on rocky shores,
And the rash hunter strangled by the boars:
1200 The new-born babe by nurses overlaid;
And the cook caught within the raging fire he
    made.
All ills of Mars his nature, flame and steel;
The gasping charioteer beneath the wheel

1186 (1147).—
    The sleere of himself yet saugh I ther,
    His herte-blood hath bathed al his heer.[1]

---

[1] Hair.

Of his own car; the ruined house that falls
And intercepts her lord betwixt the walls: 1205
The whole division that to Mars pertains,
All trades of death that deal in steel for gains
Were there: the butcher, armourer, and smith,
Who forges sharpened fauchions, or the scythe.
The scarlet conquest on a tower was placed,   1210
With shouts and soldiers' acclamations graced:
A pointed sword hung threatening o'er his head,
Sustained but by a slender twine of thread.
There saw I Mars his ides, the Capitol,
The seer in vain foretelling Caesar's fall;   1215
The last Triumvirs, and the wars they move,
And Antony, who lost the world for love.
These, and a thousand more, the fane adorn;
Their fates were painted ere the men were born,
All copied from the heavens, and ruling force   1220
Of the red star, in his revolving course.
The form of Mars high on a chariot stood,
All sheathed in arms, and gruffly looked the god:
Two geomantic figures were displayed
Above his head, a warrior and a maid,   1225

1214 (1173).—Depeynted was the slaughtre of Iulius,
          Of grete Nero, and of Antonius.

1222 (1183).
          The statue of Mars upon a carte stood,
          Armed, and loked grim as he were wood;
          And over his heed ther shynen two figures
          Of sterres, that been cleped[1] in scriptures,[2]
          That oon Puella, that other Rubeus.

---

[1]Called.   [2]Any important writings; here, books on astrology.

One when direct, and one when retrograde.
  Tired with deformities of death, I haste
To the third temple of Diana chaste.
A sylvan scene with various greens was drawn,
1230 Shades on the sides, and on the midst a lawn;
The silver Cynthia, with her nymphs around,
Pursued the flying deer, the woods with horns
    resound:
Calisto there stood manifest of shame,
And, turned a bear, the northern star became:
1235 Her son was next, and, by peculiar grace,
In the cold circle held the second place:
The stag Actæon in the stream had spied
The naked huntress, and for seeing died:
His hounds, unknowing of his change, pursue
1240 The chase, and their mistaken master slew.
Peneian Daphne too was there to see,
Apollo's love before, and now his tree.
The adjoining fane the assembled Greeks expressed,
And hunting of the Calydonian beast.
1245 Œnides' valour, and his envied prize;
The fatal power of Atalanta's eyes;
Diana's vengeance on the victor shown,
The murderess mother, and consuming son;
The Volscian queen extended on the plain,
1250 The treason punished, and the traitor slain.
The rest were various huntings, well designed,
And savage beasts destroyed, of every kind.
The graceful goddess was arrayed in green;
About her feet were little beagles seen,

That watched with upward eyes the motions of 1255
    their Queen.
Her legs were buskined, and the left before,
In act to shoot; a silver bow she bore,
And at her back a painted quiver wore.
She trod a wexing moon, that soon would wane,
And, drinking borrowed light, be filled again;   1260
With downcast eyes, as seeming to survey
The dark dominions, her alternate sway.

Theseus beheld the fanes of every god,
And thought his mighty cost was well bestowed.   1270
So princes now their poets should regard;
But few can write, and fewer can reward.
    The theatre thus raised, the lists enclosed,
And all with vast magnificence disposed,
We leave the monarch pleased, and haste to bring 1275
The knights to combat, and their arms to sing.

BOOK III

The day approached when Fortune should decide
The important enterprise, and give the bride;
For now the rivals round the world had sought,
1280 And each his number, well appointed, brought.
The nations far and near contend in choice,
And send the flower of war by public voice;
That after or before were never known
Such chiefs, as each an army seemed alone:
1285 Beside the champions, all of high degree,
Who knighthood loved, and deeds of chivalry,
Thronged to the lists, and envied to behold
The names of others, not their own, enrolled.
Nor seems it strange; for every noble knight

1285-1297 (1248-1258).—The passage in Chaucer is two
lines shorter, and less fulsome in praise of England:

> For every wight that loved chivalrye,
> And wolde, his thankes,[1] han a passant[2] name,
> Hath preyed that he mighte ben of that game;
> And wel was him, that ther-to chosen was.
> For if ther fille to-morwe swich a cas,
> Ye knowen wel, that every lusty knight,
> That loveth paramours,[3] and hath his might,
> Were it in Engelond, or elles-where,
> They wolde, hir thankes,[1] wilnen to be there.
> To fighte for a lady, *benedicite!*
> It were a lusty sighte for to see.

---

[1]Thankes is an old genitive used idiomatically and meaning he or
they being willing; it means scarcely more than *willingly* or *gladly*.
[2]Surpassing.   [3]Lovers.

Who loves the fair, and is endued with might, 1290
In such a quarrel would be proud to fight.
There breathes not scarce a man on British ground
(An isle for love and arms of old renowned)
But would have sold his life to purchase fame,
To Palamon or Arcite sent his name; 1295
And had the land selected of the best,
Half had come hence, and let the world provide
    the rest.
A hundred knights with Palamon there came,
Approved in fight, and men of mighty name;
Their arms were several, as their nations were, 1300
But furnished all alike with sword and spear.
Some wore coat-armour, imitating scale;
And next their skins were stubborn shirts of mail.
Some wore a breastplate and a light juppon,
Their horses clothed with rich caparison; 1305
Some for defence would leathern bucklers use
Of folded hides, and others shields of Pruce.
One hung a pole-axe at his saddle-bow,
And one a heavy mace to stun the foe;
One for his legs and knees provided well, 1310
With jambeux armed, and double plates of steel;
This on his helmet wore a lady's glove,
And that a sleeve embroidered by his love.
   With Palamon above the rest in place,
Lycurgus came, the surly king of Thrace; 1315
Black was his beard, and manly was his face;
The balls of his broad eyes rolled in his head,
And glared betwixt a yellow and a red;

He looked a lion with a gloomy stare,
1320 And o'er his eyebrows hung his matted hair;
Big-boned, and large of limbs, with sinews strong,
Broad-shouldered, and his arms were round and
    long.
Four milk-white bulls (the Thracian use of old)
Were yoked to draw his car of burnished gold.
1325 Upright he stood, and bore aloft his shield,
Conspicuous from afar, and overlooked the field.
His surcoat was a bear-skin on his back;
His hair hung long behind, and glossy raven-black.
His ample forehead bore a coronet,
1330 With sparkling diamonds and with rubies set.
Ten brace, and more, of greyhounds, snowy fair,
And tall as stags, ran loose, and coursed around
    his chair,
A match for pards in flight, in grappling for the
    bear;
With golden muzzles all their mouths were bound,
1335 And collars of the same their necks surround.
Thus through the fields Lycurgus took his way;
His hundred knights attend in pomp and proud
    array.
    To match this monarch, with strong Arcite came
Emetrius, king of Inde, a mighty name,
1340 On a bay courser, goodly to behold,
The trappings of his horse embossed with barbarous
    gold.
Not Mars bestrode a steed with greater grace;
His surcoat o'er his arms was cloth of Thrace,

Adorned with pearls, all orient, round, and great;
His saddle was of gold, with emeralds set;　　　1345
His shoulders large a mantle did attire,
With rubies thick, and sparkling as the fire;
His amber-coloured locks in ringlets run,
With graceful negligence, and shone against the
　　sun.
His nose was aquiline, his eyes were blue,　　　1350
Ruddy his lips, and fresh and fair his hue;
Some sprinkled freckles on his face were seen,
Whose dusk set off the whiteness of the skin.
His awful presence did the crowd surprise,
Nor durst the rash spectator meet his eyes;　　　1355
Eyes that confessed him born for kingly sway,
So fierce, they flashed intolerable day.
His age in nature's youthful prime appeared,
And just began to bloom his yellow beard.
Whene'er he spoke, his voice was heard around,　　　1360
Loud as a trumpet, with a silver sound;
A laurel wreathed his temples, fresh, and green,
And myrtle sprigs, the marks of love, were mixed
　　between.
Upon his fist he bore, for his delight,
An eagle well reclaimed, and lily white.　　　1365

1348 (1307).—
　　His crispe heer lyk ringes was y-ronne,[1]
　　And that was yelow, and glitered as the sonne.
1354 (1313).—Chaucer has only one line:
　　And as a leoun he his loking caste.
1359 (1314).—Of fyve and twenty yeer his age I caste.

---

[1]Clustered, curled.

His hundred knights attend him to the war,
All armed for battle; save their heads were bare.
Words and devices blazed on every shield,
And pleasing was the terror of the field.
1370 For kings, and dukes, and barons you might see,
Like sparkling stars, though different in degree,
All for the increase of arms, and love of chivalry.
Before the king tame leopards led the way,
And troops of lions innocently play.
1375 So Bacchus through the conquered Indies rode,
And beasts in gambols frisked before their honest
    god.
In this array the war of either side
Through Athens passed with military pride.
At prime, they entered on the Sunday morn;
1380 Rich tapestry spread the streets, and flowers the
    posts adorn.
The town was all a jubilee of feasts;
So Theseus willed in honour of his guests:
Himself with open arms the kings embraced,
Then all the rest in their degrees were graced.
1385 No harbinger was needful for the night,
For every house was proud to lodge a knight.
I pass the royal treat, nor must relate
The gifts bestowed, nor how the champions sate;
Who first, who last, or how the knights addressed
1390 Their vows, or who was fairest at the feast;
Whose voice, whose graceful dance did most sur-
    prise,
Soft amorous sighs, and silent love of eyes.

The rivals call my Muse another way,
To sing their vigils for the ensuing day.
'Twas ebbing darkness, past the noon of night: 1395
And Phosphor, on the confines of the light,
Promised the sun; ere day began to spring,
The tuneful lark already stretched her wing,
And flickering on her nest, made short essays to sing,
When wakeful Palamon, preventing day,   1400
Took to the royal lists his early way,
To Venus at her fane, in her own house, to pray.
There, falling on his knees before her shrine,
He thus implored with prayers her power divine:
"Creator Venus, genial power of love,   .   1405

1395-1404 (1351-1362).—Chaucer has twelve lines to
Dryden's ten:

> The Sonday night, er[1] day bigan to springe,
> When Palamon the larke herde singe,
> Although it nere nat[2] day by houres two,
> Yet song the larke, and Palamon also.
> With holy herte, and with an heigh corage
> He roos,[3] to wenden on his pilgrimage
> Un-to the blisful Citherea benygne,
> I mene Venus, honurable and dygne.[4]
> And in hir houre he walketh forth a pas
> Un-to the listes, ther[5] hir temple was,
> And doun he kneleth, and with humble chere
> And herte soor, he seide as ye shul[6] here.

1405 (1363).—Chaucer's invocation is much shorter:

> 'Faireste of faire, o lady myn Venus,
> Doughter to Iove, and spouse of Vulcanus,
> Thou gladere of the mount of Citheroun
> For thilke[7] love thou haddest to Adoun,[8]
> Have pitee of my bittre teres smerte,
> And tak myn humble preyere at thin herte.

---

[1]Ere.   [2]Double negative; it was not day.   [3]Rose.   [4]Latin
dignus; worthy.   [5]Where.   [6]Shall.   [7]That.   [8]Adonis.

The bliss of men below, and gods above!
Beneath the sliding sun thou runst thy race,
Dost fairest shine, and best become thy place.
For thee the winds their eastern blasts forbear,
1410 Thy month reveals the spring, and opens all the year.
Thee, Goddess, thee the storms of winter fly;
Earth smiles with flowers renewing, laughs the sky,
And birds to lays of love their tuneful notes apply.
'Tis thine, whate'er is pleasant, good, or fair;
1415 All nature is thy province, life thy care;
Thou madest the world, and dost the world repair.
Thou gladder of the mount of Cytheron,
Increase of Jove, companion of the Sun,
If e'er Adonis touched thy tender heart,
1420 Have pity, Goddess, for thou knowest the smart!
Alas! I have not words to tell my grief;
To vent my sorrow would be some relief;
Light sufferings give us leisure to complain;
We groan, but cannot speak, in greater pain.
1425 O Goddess, tell thyself what I would say!
Thou knowest it, and I feel too much to pray.
So grant my suit, as I enforce my might,
In love to be thy champion and thy knight,
A servant to thy sex, a slave to thee,
1430 A foe professed to barren chastity:
Nor ask I fame or honour of the field,
Nor choose I more to vanquish than to yield:
In my divine Emilia make me blest,
Let Fate or partial Chance dispose the rest:
1435 Find thou the manner, and the means prepare;

Possession, more than conquest, is my care.
Mars is the warrior's god; in him it lies
On whom he favours to confer the prize;
With smiling aspect you serenely move
In your fifth orb, and rule the realm of love.   1440
The Fates but only spin the coarser clue,
The finest of the wool is left for you:
Spare me but one small portion of the twine,
And let the Sisters cut below your line:
The rest among the rubbish may they sweep,   1445
Or add it to the yarn of some old miser's heap,
But if you this ambitious prayer deny,
(A wish, I grant, beyond mortality,)
Then let me sink beneath proud Arcite's arms,
And, I once dead, let him possess her charms.''   1450
    Thus ended he; then, with observance due,
The sacred incense on her altar threw:
The curling smoke mounts heavy from the fires;
At length it catches flame, and in a blaze expires;
At once the gracious Goddess gave the sign,   1455
Her statue shook, and trembled all the shrine:
Pleased Palamon the tardy omen took;
For since the flames pursued the trailing smoke,
He knew his boon was granted, but the day
To distance driven, and joy adjourned with long 1460
    delay.
    Now morn with rosy light had streaked the sky,
Up rose the sun, and up rose Emily;

1450 (1402).—Chaucer ends the prayer with the line:
    Yif me my love, thou blisful lady dere.

Addressed her early steps to Cynthia's fane,
In state attended by her maiden train,
1465 Who bore the vests that holy rites require,
Incense, and odorous gums, and covered fire.
The plenteous horns with pleasant mead they crown
Nor wanted aught besides in honour of the Moon.
Now, while the temple smoked with hallowed steam,
1470 They wash the virgin in a living stream;

Her shining hair, uncombed, was loosely spread,
1480 A crown of mastless oak adorned her head:
When to the shrine approached, the spotless maid
Had kindling fires on either altar laid;
(The rites were such as were observed of old,
By Statius in his Theban story told.)
1485 Then kneeling with her hands across her breast,
Thus lowly she preferred her chaste request.
"O Goddess, haunter of the woodland green,
To whom both heaven and earth and seas are seen;
Queen of the nether skies, where half the year
1490 Thy silver beams descend, and light the gloomy
      sphere;
Goddess of maids, and conscious of our hearts,
So keep me from the vengeance of thy darts,
(Which Niobe's devoted issue felt,
When hissing through the skies the feathered
      deaths were dealt,)

1463 (1416).—Notice the much greater simplicity of
Chaucer's line:
      And to the temple of Diane gan hye.

As I desire to live a virgin life,　　　　　　　　1495
Nor know the name of mother or of wife.
Thy votress from my tender years I am,
And love, like thee, the woods and sylvan game.
Like death, thou knowest, I loathe the nuptial
　　state.
And man, the tyrant of our sex, I hate,　　　　　1500
A lowly servant, but a lofty mate;

Now by thy triple shape, as thou art seen
In heaven, earth, hell, and everywhere a queen,　1505
Grant this my first desire; let discord cease,
And make betwixt the rivals lasting peace:
Quench their hot fire, or far from me remove
The flame, and turn it on some other love;
Or if my frowning stars have so decreed,　　　　1510
That one must be rejected, one succeed,
Make him my lord, within whose faithful breast
Is fixed my image, and who loves me best.
But oh! even that avert! I choose it not,
But take it as the least unhappy lot.　　　　　　1515
A maid I am, and of thy virgin train;
Oh, let me still that spotless name retain!
Frequent the forests, thy chaste will obey,
And only make the beasts of chase my prey!"
　　The flames ascend on either altar clear,　　　1520
While thus the blameless maid addressed her prayer.
When lo! the burning fire that shone so bright
Flew off, all sudden, with extinguished light,

1516(1472).—And whyl I live a mayde, I wol thee serve.

And left one altar dark, a little space,
1525 Which turned self-kindled, and renewed the blaze;
That other victor-flame a moment stood,
Then fell, and lifeless left the extinguished wood;
For ever lost, the irrevocable light
Forsook the blackening coals, and sunk to night:
1530 At either end it whistled as it flew,
And as the brands were green, so dropped the dew.
Infected as it fell with sweat of sanguine hue.
The maid from that ill omen turned her eyes,
And with loud shrieks and clamours rent the skies;
1535 Nor knew what signified the boding sign,
But found the powers displeased, and feared the
     wrath divine.
Then shook the sacred shrine, and sudden light
Sprung through the vaulted roof, and made the
     temple bright.
The Power, behold! the Power in glory shone,
1540 By her bent bow and her keen arrows known;
The rest, a huntress issuing from the wood,
Reclining on her cornel spear she stood.

1526 (1477).—
                         —and after that anon
     That other fyr was queynt,[1] and al agon;
    . And as it queynte, it made a whistelinge,
     As doon thise wete brondes in hir brenninge.[2]
     And at the brondes ende out-ran anoon
     As it were blody dropes many oon;
1537 (1488).—
     And ther-with-al Diane gan appere,
     With bowe in hond, right as an hunteresse,
     And seyde: 'Doghter, stint thyn hevinesse.

---

[1]Quenched.   [2]Burning.

Then gracious thus began: "Dismiss thy fear,
And Heaven's unchanged decrees attentive hear:
More powerful gods have torn thee from my side, 1545
Unwilling to resign, and doomed a bride;
The two contending knights are weighed above;
One Mars protects, and one the Queen of Love:
But which the man is in the Thunderer's breast;
This he pronounced, ' 'Tis he who loves thee best.' 1550
The fire that, once extinct, revived again
Foreshows the love allotted to remain.
Farewell!" she said, and vanished from the place;
The sheaf of arrows shook, and rattled in the case.
Aghast at this, the royal virgin stood, 1555
Disclaimed, and now no more a sister of the wood:
But to the parting Goddess thus she prayed:
"Propitious still, be present to my aid,
Nor quite abandon your once favoured maid."
Then sighing she returned; but smiled betwixt, 1560
With hopes, and fears, and joys with sorrows mixt.
  The next returning planetary hour
Of Mars, who shared the heptarchy of power,
His steps bold Arcite to the temple bent,
To adorn with pagan rites the power armipotent: 1565
Then prostrate, low before his altar lay,

1549 (1495).—But un-to which of hem I may nat telle.

1560 (1507).—
    And hoom she goth anon the nexte weye.
    This is theffect,[1] ther is namore to seye.

---

[1] The effect, the conclusion.

And raised his manly voice, and thus began to
    pray:
"Strong God of Arms, whose iron sceptre sways
The freezing North, and Hyperborean seas,
1570 And Scythian colds, and Thracia's wintry coast,
Where stand thy steeds, and thou art honoured most:
There most, but everywhere thy power is known,
The fortune of the fight is all thy own:
Terror is thine, and wild amazement, flung
1575 From out thy chariot, withers even the strong;
And disarray and shameful rout ensue,
And force is added to the fainting crew.
Acknowledged as thou art, accept my prayer!
If aught I have achieved deserve thy care,
1580 If to my utmost power with sword and shield
I dared the death, unknowing how to yield,
And falling in my rank, still kept the field;
Then let my arms prevail, by thee sustained,
That Emily by conquest may be gained.
1585 Have pity on my pains; nor those unknown
To Mars, which, when a lover, were his own.
Venus, the public care of all above,
Thy stubborn heart has softened into love:

1595 By those dear pleasures, aid my arms in fight,
And make me conquer in my patron's right:

1566 (1513).—
    With pitous[1] herte and heigh devocioun,
    Right thus to Mars he seyde his orisoun.

---

[1] Piteous, compassionate.

For I am young, a novice in the trade,
The fool of love, unpractised to persuade,
And want the soothing arts that catch the fair,
But, caught myself, lie struggling in the snare;   1600
And she I love or laughs at all my pain
Or knows her worth too well, and pays me with
    disdain.
For sure I am, unless I win in arms,
To stand excluded from Emilia's charms:
Nor can my strength avail, unless by thee   1605
Endued with force I gain the victory;
Then for the fire which warmed thy generous heart,
Pity thy subject's pains and equal smart.
So be the morrow's sweat and labour mine,
The palm and honour of the conquest thine: 1610
Then shall the war, and stern debate, and strife
Immortal be the business of my life;
And in thy fane, the dusty spoils among,
High on the burnished roof, my banner shall be hung,
Ranked with my champion's bucklers; and below,   1615
With arms reversed, the atchievements of my foe;
And while these limbs the vital spirit feeds,
While day to night, and night to day succeeds,
Thy smoking altar shall be fat with food
Of incense and the grateful steam of blood;   1620
Burnt-offerings morn and evening shall be thine,
And fires eternal in thy temple shine.
The bush of yellow beard, this length of hair,
Which from my birth inviolate I bear,
Guiltless of steel, and from the razor free,   1625

Shall fall a plenteous crop, reserved for thee.
So may my arms with victory be blest,
I ask no more; let Fate dispose the rest."
The champion ceased; there followed in the close
1630 A hollow groan; a murmuring wind arose;
The rings of iron, that on the doors were hung,
Sent out a jarring sound, and harshly rung:
The bolted gates flew open at the blast,
The storm rushed in, and Arcite stood aghast:
1635 The flames were blown aside, yet shone they bright,
Fanned by the wind, and gave a ruffled light.
Then from the ground a scent began to rise,
Sweet smelling as accepted sacrifice:
This omen pleased, and as the flames aspire
1640 With odorous incense Arcite heaps the fire:
Nor wanted hymns to Mars or heathen charms:
At length the nodding statue clashed his arms,
And with a sullen sound and feeble cry,
Half sunk and half pronounced the word of Victory.
1645 For this, with soul devout, he thanked the God,
And, of success secure, returned to his abode.
These vows, thus granted, raised a strife above
Betwixt the God of War and Queen of Love.
She, granting first, had right of time to plead;

1643 (1574).—
    And with that soun he herde a murmuringe
    Ful lowe and dim, that sayde thus, 'Victorie.'

1645 (1578).—
    Arcite anon un-to his inne is fare
    As fayn[1] as fowel[2] is of the brighte sonne.

---

[1]Glad.   [2]Bird.

But he had granted too, nor would recede.   1650
Jove was for Venus, but he feared his wife,
And seemed unwilling to decide the strife;
Till Saturn from his leaden throne arose,
And found a way the difference to compose:
Though sparing of his grace, to mischief bent,   1655
He seldom does a good with good intent.
Wayward, but wise; by long experience taught,
To please both parties, for ill ends, he sought:
For this advantage age from youth has won,
As not to be outridden, though outrun.   1660
By fortune he was now to Venus trined,
And with stern Mars in Capricorn was joined:
Of him disposing in his own abode,
He soothed the Goddess, while he gulled the God:
"Cease, daughter, to complain, and stint the strife;   1665
Thy Palamon shall have his promised wife:
And Mars, the lord of conquest, in the fight
With palm and laurel shall adorn his knight.
Wide is my course, nor turn I to my place
Till length of time, and move with tardy pace.   1670
Man feels me, when I press the ethereal plains;
My hand is heavy, and the wound remains.
Mine is the shipwreck in a watery sign;
And in an earthy the dark dungeon mine.
Cold shivering agues, melancholy care,   1675
And bitter blasting winds, and poisoned air,

1659 (1591).—
      Men may the olde at-renne, and noght at-rede.[1]

---

[1] The young may outrun the old, but not surpass them in counsel.

Are mine, and wilful death, resulting from despair.
The throttling quinsey 'tis my star appoints,
And rheumatisms I send to rack the joints:
1680 When churls rebel against their native prince,
I arm their hands, and furnish the pretence;
And housing in the lion's hateful sign,
Bought senates and deserting troops are mine.
Mine is the privy poisoning; I command
1685 Unkindly seasons and ungrateful land.
By me kings' palaces are pushed to ground,
And miners crushed beneath their mines are found.
'Twas I slew Samson, when the pillared hall
Fell down, and crushed the many with the fall.
1690 My looking is the sire of pestilence,
That sweeps at once the people and the prince.
Now weep no more, but trust thy grandsire's art,
Mars shall be pleased, and thou perform thy part.
'Tis ill, though different your complexions are,
1695 The family of Heaven for men should war.''
The expedient pleased, where neither lost his right;
Mars had the day, and Venus had the night.
The management they left to Chronos' care;
Now turn we to the effect, and sing the war.
1700   In Athens all was pleasure, mirth, and play,
All proper to the spring, and sprightly May:
Which every soul inspired with such delight,
'Twas justing all the day, and love at night.
Heaven smiled, and gladded was the heart of man;
1705 And Venus had the world as when it first began.
At length in sleep their bodies they compose,

And dreamt the future fight, and early rose.
   Now scarce the dawning day began to spring,
As at a signal given, the streets with clamours ring:
At once the crowd arose; confused and high,   1710
Even from the heaven was heard a shouting cry,
For Mars was early up, and roused the sky.
The gods came downward to behold the wars,
Sharpening their sights, and leaning from their
     stars.
The neighing of the generous horse was heard,   1715
For battle by the busy groom prepared:
Rustling of harness, rattling of the shield,
Clattering of armour, furbished for the field.
Crowds to the castle mounted up the street;
Battering the pavement with their coursers' feet: 1720
The greedy sight might there devour the gold
Of glittering arms, too dazzling to behold:
And polished steel that cast the view aside,
And crested morions, with their plumy pride.
Knights, with a long retinue of their squires,   1725
In gaudy liveries march, and quaint attires.
One laced the helm, another held the lance;
A third the shining buckler did advance.
The courser pawed the ground with restless feet,
And snorting foamed, and champed the golden bit. 1730
The smiths and armourers on palfreys ride,
Files in their hands, and hammers at their side,
And nails for loosened spears, and thongs for
     shields provide.
The yeomen guard the streets in seemly bands;

1735 And clowns come crowding on, with cudgels in
    their hands.
    The trumpets, next the gate, in order placed,
    Attend the sign to sound the martial blast:
    The palace-yard is filled with floating tides,
    And the last comers bear the former to the sides.
1740 The throng is in the midst; the common crew
    Shut out, the hall admits the better few.
    In knots they stand, or in a rank they walk,
    Serious in aspect, earnest in their talk;
    Factious, and favouring this or t'other side,
1745 As their strong fancies and weak reason guide:
    Their wagers back their wishes; numbers hold
    With the fair freckled king, and beard of gold:
    So vigorous are his eyes, such rays they cast,
    So prominent his eagle's beak is placed.
1750 But most their looks on the black monarch bend,
    His rising muscles and his brawn commend;
    His double-biting axe, and beamy spear,
    Each asking a gigantic force to rear.
    All spoke as partial favour moved the mind;
1755 And, safe themselves, at others' cost divined.
    Waked by the cries, the Athenian chief arose,
    The knightly forms of combat to dispose;
    And passing through the obsequious guards, he sate
    Conspicuous on a throne, sublime in state;

1736 (1653).—
        Pypes, trompes, nakers,[1] clariounes,
        That in the bataille blowen blody sounes.[2]

---

[1] Kettle-drums.   [2] Sounds.

There, for the two contending knights he sent;   1760
Armed cap-a-pe, with reverence low they bent:
He smiled on both, and with superior look
Alike their offered adoration took.
The people press on every side to see
Their awful Prince, and hear his high decree.   1765
Then signing to their heralds with his hand,
They gave his orders from their lofty stand.
Silence is thrice enjoined; then thus aloud
The king-at-arms bespeaks the knights and listening
    crowd:
"Our sovereign lord has pondered in his mind   1770
The means to spare the blood of gentle kind;
And of his grace and inborn clemency,
He modifies his first severe decree,
The keener edge of battle to rebate,
The troops for honour fighting, not for hate.   1775
He wills, not death should terminate their strife,
And wounds, if wounds ensue, be short of life;
But issues, ere the fight, his dread command,
That slings afar, and poniards hand to hand,
Be banished from the field; that none shall dare   1780
With shortened sword to stab in closer war;
But in fair combat fight with manly strength,

1758 (1670).—
    Duk Theseus was at a window set,
    Arrayed right as he were a god in trone.[1]

1771 (1683).—
    Wherfore, to shapen[2] that they shul not dye,
    Ie wol his firste purpos modifye.

---

 [1] On a throne.   [2] Make sure.

Nor push with biting point, but strike at length.
The turney is allowed but one career
1785 Of the tough ash, with the sharp-grinded spear,
But knights unhorsed may rise from off the plain,
And fight on foot their honour to regain;
Nor, if at mischief taken, on the ground
Be slain, but prisoners to the pillar bound,
1790 At either barrier placed; nor, captives made,
Be freed, or armed anew the fight invade:
The chief of either side, bereft of life,
Or yielded to his foe, concludes the strife.
Thus dooms the lord: now valiant knights and
    young,
1795 Fight each his fill, with swords and maces long."
    The herald ends: the vaulted firmament
With loud acclaims and vast applause is rent:
Heaven guard a Prince so gracious and so good,
So just, and yet so provident of blood!
1800 This was the general cry. The trumpets sound,
And warlike symphony is heard around.
The marching troops through Athens take their
    way,
The great Earl-marshal orders their array.
The fair from high the passing pomp behold;
1805 A rain of flowers is from the windows rolled.

1796 (1703).—
    The voys of peple touchede the hevene,
    So loude cryden they with mery stevene[1]:
    'God save swich a lord, that is so good,
    He wilneth no destruccioun of blood.'

---

[1] Sound.

The casements are with golden tissue spread,
And horses' hoofs, for earth, on silken tapestry
    tread.
The King goes midmost, and the rivals ride
In equal rank, and close his either side.
Next after these there rode the royal wife,   1810
With Emily, the cause and the reward of strife.
The following cavalcade, by three and three,
Proceed by titles marshalled in degree.
Thus through the southern gate they take their
    way,
And at the list arrived ere prime of day.   1815
There, parting from the King, the chiefs divide,
And wheeling east and west, before their many ride.
The Athenian monarch mounts his throne on high,
And after him the Queen and Emily:
Next these, the kindred of the crown are graced   1820
With nearer seats, and lords by ladies placed.
Scarce were they seated, when with clamours loud
In rushed at once a rude promiscuous crowd,
The guards, and then each other overbare,
And in a moment throng the spacious theatre.   1825
Now changed the jarring noise to whispers low,
As winds forsaking seas more softly blow,
When at the western gate, on which the car
Is placed aloft that bears the God of War,
Proud Arcite entering armed before his train   1830
Stops at the barrier, and divides the plain.
Red was his banner, and displayed abroad
The bloody colours of his patron god.

At that self moment enters Palamon,
1835 The gate of Venus, and the rising Sun;
Waved by the wanton winds, his banner flies,
All maiden white, and shares the people's eyes.
From east to west, look all the world around,
Two troops so matched were never to be found;
1840 Such bodies built for strength, of equal age,
In stature sized; so proud an equipage:
The nicest eye could no distinction make,
Where lay the advantage, or what side to take.
Thus ranged, the herald for the last proclaims
1845 A silence, while they answered to their names:
For so the king decreed, to shun with care
The fraud of musters false, the common bane of
war.
The tale was just, and then the gates were closed;
And chief to chief, and troop to troop opposed.
1850 The heralds last retired, and loudly cried,
"The fortune of the field be fairly tried!"
At this the challenger, with fierce defy
His trumpet sounds; the challenged makes reply:
With clangour rings the field, resounds the vaulted
sky.
1855 Their vizors closed, their lances in the rest,
Or at the helmet pointed, or the crest,
They vanish from the barrier, speed the race,
And spurring see decrease the middle space.

1851 (1740).—
Do now your devoir,[1] yonge knightes proude!

---

[1] French word meaning duty.

A cloud of smoke envelopes either host,
And all at once the combatants are lost: 1860
Darkling they join adverse, and shock unseen,
Coursers with coursers justling, men with men:
As labouring in eclipse, a while they stay,
Till the next blast of wind restores the day.
They look anew; the beauteous form of fight   1865
Is changed, and war appears a grisly sight.
Two troops in fair array one moment showed,
The next, a field with fallen bodies strowed:
Not half the number in their seats are found;
But men and steeds lie grovelling on the ground. 1870
The points of spears are stuck within the shield,
The steeds without their riders scour the field.
The knights unhorsed, on foot renew the fight;
The glittering fauchions cast a gleaming light:
Hauberks and helms are hewed with many a 1875
        wound,
Out spins the streaming blood, and dyes the ground.
The mighty maces with such haste descend,

1871 (1748).—
    He feleth thurgh the herte-spoon[1] the prikke.
    Up springen speres twenty foot on highte;
    Out goth the swerdes as the silver brighte.
    The helmes they to-hewen[2] and to-shrede;[3]
    Out brest the blood, with sterne stremes rede.
    With mighty maces the bones they to-breste.[4]
    He thurgh the thikkeste of the throng gan
        threste.
    Ther stomblen steedes stronge, and doun goth
        alle.
    He rolleth under foot as doth a balle.

---

[1]Lower part of breast.   [2]Hewed.   [3]Cut in shreds.   [4]Break.

They break the bones, and make the solid armour
    bend.
This thrusts amid the throng with furious force;
1880 Down goes, at once, the horseman and the horse:
That courser stumbles on the fallen steed,
And, floundering, throws the rider o'er his head.
One rolls along, a football to his foes;
One with a broken truncheon deals his blows.
1885 This halting, this disabled with his wound,
In triumph led, is to the pillar bound,
Where by the king's award he must abide:
There goes a captive led on t'other side.
By fits they cease, and leaning on the lance,
1890 Take breath awhile, and to new fight advance.
    Full oft the rivals met, and neither spared
His utmost force, and each forgot to ward:
The head of this was to the saddle bent,
The other backward to the crupper sent:
1895 Both were by turns unhorsed; the jealous blows
Fall thick and heavy, when on foot they close.
So deep their fauchions bite, that every stroke
Pierced to the quick; and equal wounds they gave
    and took.
Borne far asunder by the tides of men,
1900 Like adamant and steel they met agen.
    So when a tiger sucks the bullock's blood,
A famished lion issuing from the wood
Roars lordly fierce, and challenges the food.
Each claims possession, neither will obey,
1905 But both their paws are fastened on the prey;

They bite, they tear; and while in vain they strive,
The swains come armed between, and both to
    distance drive.
  At length, as Fate foredoomed, and all things
    tend
By course of time to their appointed end;
So when the sun to west was far declined,   1910
And both afresh in mortal battle joined,
The strong Emetrius came in Arcite's aid,
And Palamon with odds was overlaid:
For, turning short, he struck with all his might
Full on the helmet of the unwary knight.   1915
Deep was the wound; he staggered with the blow,
And turned him to his unexpected foe;
Whom with such force he struck, he felled him
    down,
And cleft the circle of his golden crown.
But Arcite's men, who now prevailed in fight,   1920
Twice ten at once surround the single knight:
O'erpowered at length, they force him to the
    ground,
Unyielded as he was, and to the pillar bound;
And king Lycurgus, while he fought in vain
His friend to free, was tumbled on the plain.   1925
  Who now laments but Palamon, compelled
No more to try the fortune of the field,
And, worse than death, to view with hateful eyes
His rival's conquest, and renounce the prize!
  The royal judge on his tribunal placed,   1930
Who had beheld the fight from first to last,

Bad cease the war; pronouncing from on high,
Arcite of Thebes had won the beauteous Emily.
The sound of trumpets to the voice replied,
1935 And round the royal lists the heralds cried,
"Arcite of Thebes has won the beauteous bride!"
   The people rend the skies with vast applause;
All own the chief, when Fortune owns the cause.
Arcite is owned even by the gods above,
1940 And conquering Mars insults the Queen of Love.
So laughed he when the rightful Titan failed,
And Jove's usurping arms in heaven prevailed.
Laughed all the powers who favour tyranny,
And all the standing army of the sky.
1945 But Venus with dejected eyes appears,
And weeping on the lists distilled her tears;
Her will refused, which grieves a woman most,
And, in her champion foiled, the cause of Love is
      lost.
Till Saturn said:—"Fair daughter, now be still,
1950 The blustering fool has satisfied his will;
His boon is given; his knight has gained the day,
But lost the prize; the arrears are yet to pay.
Thy hour is come, and mine the care shall be
To please thy knight, and set thy promise free."

1936 (1800).—
      'Arcite of Thebes shal have Emelye,
      That by his fortune hath hir faire y-wonne.'
      Anon ther is a noyse of peple bygonne[1]
      For Ioye of this, so lowde and heigh with-alle,
      It semed that the listes sholde falle.

---

[1] Begun.

Now while the heralds run the lists around,   1955
And Arcite! Arcite! heaven and earth resound,
A miracle (nor less it could be called)
Their joy with unexpected sorrow palled.
The victor knight had laid his helm aside,
Part for his ease, the greater part for pride: 1960
Bareheaded, popularly low he bowed,
And paid the salutations of the crowd;
Then spurring, at full speed, ran endlong on
Where Theseus sat on his imperial throne;
Furious he drove, and upward cast his eye, •   1965
Where, next the Queen, was placed his Emily;
Then pausing, to the saddle-bow he bent;•
A sweet regard the gracious virgin lent;
(For women, to the brave an easy prey,
Still follow Fortune, where she leads the way:)   1970
Just then from earth sprung out a flashing fire,
By Pluto sent, at Saturn's bad desire:
The startling steed was seized with sudden fright,
And, bounding, o'er the pummel cast the knight;
Forward he flew, and pitching on his head,   1975
He quivered with his feet, and lay for dead.
Black was his countenance in a little space,
For all the blood was gathered in his face.
Help was at hand: they reared him from the
        ground,
And from his cumbrous arms his limbs unbound; 1980
Then lanced a vein, and watched returning breath;
It came, but clogged with symptoms of his death.
The saddle-bow the noble parts had prest,

All bruised and mortified his manly breast.
1985 Him still entranced, and in a litter laid,
They bore from field, and to his bed conveyed.
At length he waked; and, with a feeble cry,
The word he first pronounced, was Emily.
 Mean time the King, though inwardly he mourned,
1990 In pomp triumphant to the town returned,
Attended by the chiefs who fought the field,
(Now friendly mixed, and in one troop compelled,)
Composed his looks to counterfeited cheer,
And bade them not for Arcite's life to fear.
1995 But that which gladded all the warrior train,
Though most were sorely wounded, none were slain.
The surgeons soon despoiled them of their arms,
And some with salves they cure, and some with charms;
Foment the bruises, and the pains assuage,
2000 And heal their inward hurts with sovereign draughts of sage.
The King in person visits all around,
Comforts the sick, congratulates the sound;
Honours the princely chiefs, rewards the rest,
And holds for thrice three days a royal feast.
2005 None was disgraced; for falling is no shame,
And cowardice alone is loss of fame.

1986 (1836).—Anon he was y-born out of the place
    With herte soor, to Theseus paleys.[1]
2003 (1877).—And yaf hem yiftes after hir degree,
    And fully heeld a feste dayes three.

---

[1] Palace.

The venturous knight is from the saddle thrown,
But 'tis the fault of fortune, not his own;
If crowds and palms the conquering side adorn,
The victor under better stars was born: 2010
The brave man seeks not popular applause,
Nor, overpowered with arms, deserts his cause;
Unshamed, though foiled, he does the best he can:
Force is of brutes, but honour is of man.
 Thus Theseus smiled on all with equal grace,   2015
And each was set according to his place;
With ease were reconciled the differing parts,
For envy never dwells in noble hearts.
At length they took their leave, the time expired;
Well pleased, and to their several homes retired.   2020
 Meanwhile, the health of Arcite still impairs;
From bad proceeds to worse, and mocks the
  leech's cares;
Swoln is his breast; his inward pains increase;
All means are used, and all without success.
The clottered blood lies heavy on his heart,   2025
Corrupts, and there remains in spite of art;
Nor breathing veins nor cupping will prevail;
All outward remedies and inward fail.
The mould of nature's fabric is destroyed,
Her vessels discomposed, her virtue void: 2030
The bellows of his lungs begins to swell;
All out of frame is every secret cell,
Nor can the good receive, nor bad expel.
Those breathing organs, thus within opprest,
With venom soon distend the sinews of his breast.   2035

Nought profits him to save abandoned life,
Nor vomit's upward aid, nor downward laxative.
The midmost region battered and destroyed,
When nature cannot work, the effect of art is void:
2040 For physic can but mend our crazy state,
Patch an old building, not a new create.
Arcite is doomed to die in all his pride,
Must leave his youth and yield his beauteous bride,
Gained hardly against right, and unenjoyed.
2045 When 'twas declared all hope of life was past,
Conscience, that of all physic works the last,
Caused him to send for Emily in haste.
With her, at his desire, came Palamon;
Then, on his pillow raised, he thus begun:
2050 "No language can express the smallest part
Of what I feel, and suffer in my heart,
For you, whom best I love and value most;
But to your service I bequeath my ghost;
Which, from this mortal body when untied,

2050 (1907).—
    'Naught may the woful spirit in myn herte
    Declare o[1] poynt of alle my sorwes smerte
    To yow, my lady, that I love most;
    But I byquethe the service of my gost[2]
    To yow aboven every creature,
    Sin that my lyf ne may no lenger dure.[3]
    Allas, the wo! allas, the peynes stronge,
    That I for yow have suffred, and so longe!
    Allas, the deeth! allas, myn Emelye!
    Allas, departing of our compaignye!
    Allas, myn hertes quene! allas, my wyf!
    Myn hertes lady, endere of my lyf!
    What is this world? what asketh men to have?

---

[1]One.　[2]Ghost, spirit.　[3]Endure.

Unseen, unheard, shall hover at your side;   2055
Nor fright you waking, nor your sleep offend,
But wait officious, and your steps attend.
How I have loved, excuse my faltering tongue,
My spirit's feeble, and my pains are strong:
This I may say, I only grieve to die,   2060
Because I lose my charming Emily.
To die, when Heaven had put you in my power!
Fate could not choose a more malicious hour.
What greater curse could envious Fortune give,
Than just to die when I began to live!   2065
Vain men! how vanishing a bliss we crave;

Now with his love, now in his colde grave,
Allone, with-outen any compaignye.
Fare-wel, my swete fo![1] myn Emelye!
And softe tak me in your armes tweye,
For love of God, and herkneth what I seye.
   I have heer with my cosin Palamon
Had stryf and rancour, many a day a-gon,
For love of yow, and for my Ielousye.
And Iupiter so wis my soule gye,[2]
To speken of a servant proprely,
With alle circumstaunces trewely,
That is to seyn,[3] trouthe, honour, and knighthede,
Wisdom, humblesse, estaat,[4] and heigh kinrede,[5]
Fredom, and al that longeth[6] to that art,
So Iupiter have of my soule part,
As in this world right now ne knowe I non
So worthy to be loved as Palamon,
That serveth yow, and wol doon al his lyf.
And if that evere ye shul been a wyf,
Foryet nat Palamon, the gentil man.'
And with that word his speche faille gan,
For fro his feet up to his brest was come
The cold of deeth, that hadde him overcome.

---

[1]Foe.   [2]And may Jupiter so wisely guide my soul that I may
speak, etc.   [3]That there is to be seen.   [4]Possessions.   [5]High
kindred.   [6]Belongeth.

Now warm in love, now withering in the grave!
Never, O never more to see the sun!
Still dark, in a damp vault, and still alone!
2070 This fate is common; but I lose my breath
Near bliss, and yet not blessed before my death.
Farewell! but take me dying in your arms;
'Tis all I can enjoy of all your charms:
This hand I cannot but in death resign;
2075 Ah, could I live! but while I live 'tis mine.
I feel my end approach and thus embraced
Am pleased to die; but hear me speak my last:
Ah, my sweet foe! for you, and you alone,
I broke my faith with injured Palamon.
2080 But love the sense of right and wrong confounds;
Strong love and proud ambition have no bounds.
And much I doubt, should Heaven my life pro-
    long,
I should return to justify my wrong;
For while my former flames remain within,
2085 Repentance is but want of power to sin.
With mortal hatred I pursued his life,
Nor he nor you were guilty of the strife;
Nor I, but as I loved; yet all combined,
Your beauty and my impotence of mind,
2090 And his concurrent flame that blew my fire,
For still our kindred souls had one desire.
He had a moment's right in point of time;
Had I seen first, then his had been the crime.
Fate made it mine, and justified his right;
2095 Nor holds this earth a more deserving knight

For virtue, valour, and for noble blood,
Truth, honour, all that is comprised in good;
So help me Heaven, in all the world is none
So worthy to be loved as Palamon.
He loves you too, with such a holy fire,   2100
As will not, cannot, but with life expire:
Our vowed affections both have often tried,
Nor any love but yours could ours divide.
Then, by my love's inviolable band,
By my long suffering and my short command,   2105
If e'er you plight your vows when I am gone,
Have pity on the faithful Palamon.''

　　This was his last; for Death came on amain,
And exercised below his iron reign;
Then upward to the seat of life he goes;   2110
Sense fled before him, what he touched he froze:
Yet could he not his closing eyes withdraw,
Though less and less of Emily he saw;
So, speechless, for a little space he lay;
Then grasped the hand he held, and sighed his 2115
　　soul away.

　　But whither went his soul? let such relate
Who search the secrets of the future state:
Divines can say but what themselves believe;
Strong proofs they have, but not demonstrative;
For, were all plain, then all sides must agree,   2120
And faith itself be lost in certainty.

2115 (1950).—
　　　His laste word was 'mercy, Emelye!'
　　　His spirit chaunged hous, and wente ther,
　　　As I cam nevere, I can nat tellen wher.

To live uprightly then is sure the best;
To save ourselves, and not to damn the rest.
The soul of Arcite went where heathens go,
2125 Who better live than we though less they know.
    In Palamon a manly grief appears;
Silent he wept, ashamed to show his tears.
Emilia shrieked but once; and then, opprest
With sorrow, sunk upon her lover's breast:
2130 Till Theseus in his arms conveyed with care
Far from so sad a sight the swooning fair.
'Twere loss of time her sorrow to relate;
Ill bears the sex a youthful lover's fate,
When just approaching to the nuptial state:
2135 But like a low-hung cloud, it rains so fast,
That all at once it falls, and cannot last.
The face of things is changed, and Athens now,
That laughed so late, becomes the scene of woe:
Matrons and maids, both sexes, every state,
2140 With tears lament the knight's untimely fate.
Not greater grief in falling Troy was seen
For Hector's death; but Hector was not then.
Old men with dust deformed their hoary hair;
The women beat their breasts, their cheeks they
    tear.
2145 "Why wouldst thou go," with one consent they
    cry,
"When thou hadst gold enough, and Emily?"
    Theseus himself, who should have cheered the
    grief
Of others, wanted now the same relief:

Old Ægeus only could revive his son,
Who various changes of the world had known,   2150
And strange vicissitudes of human fate,
Still altering, never in a steady state;
Good after ill and after pain delight,
Alternate, like the scenes of day and night.
Since every man who lives is born to die,   2155
And none can boast sincere felicity,
With equal mind, what happens, let us bear,
Nor joy, nor grieve too much for things beyond
    our care.
Like pilgrims to the appointed place we tend;
The world's an inn, and death the journey's end.   2160
Even kings but play, and when their part is done,
Some other, worse or better, mount the throne.
With words like these the crowd was satisfied;
And so they would have been, had Theseus died.
But he, their King, was labouring in his mind   2165
A fitting place for funeral pomps to find,
Which were in honour of the dead designed.
And, after long debate, at last he found
(As Love itself had marked the spot of ground,)
That grove for ever green, that conscious laund,   2170
Where he with Palamon fought hand to hand;
That, where he fed his amorous desires
With soft complaints, and felt his hottest fires,
There other flames might waste his earthly part,

2159 (1989).—
    This world nis but a thurghfare ful of wo,
    And we ben pilgrimes, passinge to and fro;
    Deeth is an ende of every worldly sore.

2175 And burn his limbs, where love had burned his
    heart.

This once resolved, the peasants were enjoined
Sere-wood, and firs, and doddered oaks to find.
With sounding axes to the grove they go,
Fell, split, and lay the fuel in a row;
2180 Vulcanian food: a bier is next prepared,
On which the lifeless body should be reared,
Covered with cloth of gold; on which was laid
The corps of Arcite, in like robes arrayed.
White gloves were on his hands, and on his head
2185 A wreath of laurel, mixed with myrtle, spread.
A sword keen-edged within his right he held,
The warlike emblem of the conquered field:
Bare was his manly visage on the bier;
Menaced his countenance, even in death severe.
2190 Then to the palace-hall they bore the knight,
To lie in solemn state, a public sight:
Groans, cries, and howlings fill the crowded place,
And unaffected sorrow sat on every face.
Sad Palamon above the rest appears,
2195 In sable garments, dewed with gushing tears;
His auburn locks on either shoulder flowed,
Which to the funeral of his friend he vowed;
But Emily, as chief, was next his side,
A virgin-widow and a mourning bride.

2188 (2019).—
      He[1] leyde him bare the visage on the bere,
      Therwith he weep that pitee was to here.

---

[1] Theseus.

And, that the princely obsequies might be   2200
Performed according to his high degree,
The steed, that bore him living to the fight,
Was trapped with polished steel, all shining
    bright,
And covered with the atchievements of the knight.
The riders rode abreast; and one his shield,   2205
His lance of cornel-wood another held;
The third his bow, and glorious to behold,
The costly quiver, all of burnished gold.
The noblest of the Grecians next appear,
And weeping on their shoulders bore the bier;   2210
With sober pace they marched, and often stayed,
And through the master-street the corps conveyed.
The houses to their tops with black were spread,
And even the pavements were with mourning hid.
The right side of the pall old Ægeus kept,   2215
And on the left the royal Theseus wept;
Each bore a golden bowl of work divine,
With honey filled, and milk, and mixed with
    ruddy wine.
Then Palamon the kinsman of the slain,
And after him appeared the illustrious train.   2220
To grace the pomp came Emily the bright,
With covered fire, the funeral pile to light.
With high devotion was the service made,
And all the rites of pagan honour paid:
So lofty was the pile, a Parthian bow,   2225
With vigour drawn, must send the shaft below.
The bottom was full twenty fathom broad,

With crackling straw beneath in due proportion
    strowed.
The fabric seemed a wood of rising green,
2230 With sulphur and bitumen cast between
To feed the flames: the trees were unctuous fir,
And mountain-ash, the mother of the spear;
The mourner-yew, and builder-oak were there,
The beech, the swimming alder, and the plane,
2235 Hard box, and linden of a softer grain,
And laurels, which the gods for conquering chiefs
    ordain.
How they were ranked shall rest untold by me,
With nameless Nymphs that lived in every tree;
Nor how the Dryads and the woodland train,
2240 Disherited, ran howling o'er the plain:
Nor how the birds to foreign seats repaired,
Or beasts that bolted out and saw the forest bared:
Nor how the ground now cleared with ghastly
    fright
Beheld the sudden sun, a stranger to the light.
2245   The straw, as first I said, was laid below:
Of chips and sere-wood was the second row;
The third of greens, and timber newly felled;
The fourth high stage the fragrant odours held,
And pearls, and precious stones, and rich array,
2250 In midst of which, embalmed, the body lay.

2241 (2071).—
    Ne how the bestes and the briddes[1] alle
    Fledden for fere, whan the wode was falle.

---

[1] Birds.

The service sung, the maid with mourning eyes
The stubble fired; the smouldering flames arise:
This office done, she sunk upon the ground;
But what she spoke, recovered from her swound,
I want the wit in moving words to dress;   2255
But by themselves the tender sex may guess.
While the devouring fire was burning fast,
Rich jewels in the flame the wealthy cast;
And some their shields, and some their lances
    threw,
And gave the warrior's ghost a warrior's due.   2260
Full bowls of wine, of honey, milk and blood
Were poured upon the pile of burning wood,
And hissing flames receive, and hungry lick the
    food.
Then thrice the mounted squadrons ride around
The fire, and Arcite's name they thrice resound: 2265
"Hail and farewell!" they shouted thrice amain,
Thrice facing to the left, and thrice they turned
    again:
Still, as they turned, they beat their clattering
    shields;
The women mix their cries; and clamour fills the
    fields.
The warlike wakes continued all the night,   2270
And funeral games were played at new returning
    light:
Who naked wrestled best, besmeared with oil,
Or who with gauntlets gave or took the foil,
I will not tell you, nor would you attend;

2275 But briefly haste to my long story's end.

I pass the rest; the year was fully mourned,
And Palamon long since to Thebes returned:
When, by the Grecians' general consent,
At Athens Theseus held his parliament;
2280 Among the laws that passed, it was decreed,
That conquered Thebes from bondage should be
freed;
Reserving homage to the Athenian throne,
To which the sovereign summoned Palamon.
Unknowing of the cause, he took his way,
2285 Mournful in mind, and still in black array.

The monarch mounts the throne, and, placed on
high,
Commands into the court the beauteous Emily.
So called, she came; the senate rose, and paid
Becoming reverence to the royal maid.
2290 And first, soft whispers through the assembly
went;
With silent wonder then they watched the event;
All hushed, the King arose with awful grace;
Deep thought was in his breast, and counsel in his
face:
At length he sighed, and having first prepared
2295 The attentive audience, thus his will declared:

"The Cause and Spring of motion from above
Hung down on earth the golden chain of Love;
Great was the effect, and high was his intent,
When peace among the jarring seeds he sent;
2300 Fire, flood, and earth and air by this were bound,

And Love, the common link, the new creation
　　crowned.
The chain still holds; for though the forms decay,
Eternal matter never wears away:
The same first mover certain bounds has placed,
How long those perishable forms shall last; 2305
Nor can they last beyond the time assigned
By that all-seeing and all-making Mind:
Shorten their hours they may, for will is free,
But never pass the appointed destiny.
To men oppressed, when weary of their breath, 2310
Throw off the burden, and suborn their death.
Then, since those forms begin, and have their end,
On some unaltered cause they sure depend:
Parts of the whole are we, but God the whole,
Who gives us life, and animating soul. 2315
For Nature cannot from a part derive
That being which the whole can only give:
He perfect, stable; but imperfect we,
Subject to change, and different in degree;
Plants, beasts, and man; and, as our organs are, 2320
We more or less of his perfection share.
But, by a long descent the ethereal fire
Corrupts; and forms, the mortal part, expire.
As he withdraws his virtue, so they pass
And the same matter makes another mass: 2325

2300 (2133).—
　　For with that faire cheyne of love he bond
　　The fyr, the eyr, the water, and the lond
　　In certeyn boundes, that they may nat flee.

This law the omniscient Power was pleased to
    give,
That every kind should by succession live;
That individuals die, his will ordains;
The propagated species still remains.
2330 The monarch oak, the patriarch of the trees,
Shoots rising up, and spreads by slow degrees;
Three centuries he grows, and three he stays,
Supreme in state, and in three more decays:
So wears the paving pebble in the street,
2335 And towns and towers their fatal periods meet:
So rivers, rapid once, now naked lie,
Forsaken of their springs, and leave their
    channels dry.

Man struggles into breath, and cries for aid;
Then helpless in his mother's lap is laid.
He creeps, he walks, and issuing into man,
2345 Grudges their life from whence his own began;
Reckless of laws, affects to rule alone,
Anxious to reign, and restless on the throne:
First vegetive, then feels, and reasons last;
Rich of three souls, and lives all three to waste.
2350 Some thus; but thousands more in flower of age,
For few arrive to run the latter stage.
Sunk in the first, in battle some are slain,
And others whelmed beneath the stormy main.
What makes all this, but Jupiter the king,
2355 At whose command we perish, and we spring?
Then 'tis our best, since thus ordained to die,

To make a virtue of necessity;
Take what he gives, since to rebel is vain;
The bad grows better, which we well sustain;
And could we choose the time, and choose aright, 2360
'Tis best to die, our honour at the height.
When we have done our ancestors no shame,
But served our friends, and well secured our fame;
Then should we wish our happy life to close,
And leave no more for fortune to dispose; 2365
So should we make our death a glad relief
From future shame, from sickness, and from grief;
Enjoying while we live the present hour,
And dying in our excellence and flower.
Then round our death-bed every friend should run, 2370
And joy us of our conquest early won;
While the malicious world, with envious tears,
Should grudge our happy end, and wish it theirs.
Since then our Arcite is with honour dead,
Why should we mourn, that he so soon is freed, 2375
Or call untimely what the gods decreed?
With grief as just a friend may be deplored,
From a foul prison to free air restored.
Ought he to thank his kinsman or his wife,
Could tears recall him into wretched life? 2380
Their sorrow hurts themselves; on him is lost,
And worse than both, offends his happy ghost.
What then remains, but after past annoy
To take the good vicissitude of joy;
To thank the gracious gods for what they give, 2385
Possess our souls, and, while we live, to live?

Ordain we then two sorrows to combine,
And in one point the extremes of grief to join;
That thence resulting joy may be renewed,
2390 As jarring notes in harmony conclude.
Then I propose that Palamon shall be
In marriage joined with beauteous Emily;
For which already I have gained the assent
Of my free people in full parliament.
2395 Long love to her has borne the faithful knight,
And well deserved, had Fortune done him right:
'Tis time to mend her fault, since Emily
By Arcite's death from former vows is free;
If you, fair sister, ratify the accord,
2400 And take him for your husband and your lord,
'Tis no dishonour to confer your grace
On one descended from a royal race;
And were he less, yet years of service past
From grateful souls exact reward at last.
2405 Pity is Heaven's and yours; nor can she find
A throne so soft as in a woman's mind."
He said; she blushed; and as o'erawed by might,
Seemed to give Theseus what she gave the
knight.
Then, turning to the Theban, thus he said:
2410 "Small arguments are needful to persuade
Your temper to comply with my command:"
And speaking thus, he gave Emilia's hand.

2387 (2213).—I rede that we make, of sorwes two,
O parfyt Ioye, lasting evere-mo.[1]

---

[1] More.

Smiled Venus, to behold her own true knight
Obtain the conquest, though he lost the fight.

All of a tenor was their after-life,   2420
No day discoloured with domestic strife;
No jealousy, but mutual truth believed,
Secure repose, and kindness undeceived.
Thus Heaven, beyond the compass of his thought,
Sent him the blessing he so dearly bought.   2425
    So may the Queen of Love long duty bless,
And all true lovers find the same success.

2413 (2239).—
    And thus with alle blisse and melodye
    Hath Palamon y-wedded Emelye.
    And God, that al this wyde world hath wroght,
    Sende him his love, that hath it dere a-boght.
    For now is Palamon in alle wele,
    Living in blisse, in richesse, and in hele;[1]
    And Emelye him loveth so tendrely,
    And he hir serveth al-so gentilly,
    That nevere was ther no word hem bitwene
    Of Ielousye, or any other tene.[2]
    Thus endeth Palamon and Emelye.
    And God save al this faire compaignye!

---

[1] Health.   [2] Annoyance.

NOTES ON DRYDEN'S DEDICATION TO THE DUCHESS OF ORMOND

It was the fashion in Dryden's time, as it had been the fashion for years before and continued to be for years afterward, for poets to dedicate their writings to the sovereign or to some great noble. Men who wrote were not as well paid and therefore not as independent in the old times as now. They were brought into notice by the praise of some great man to whom they had dedicated a book or essay or poem, and they were often supported by the money which great men paid for these dedications. Therefore authors were tempted to be fulsome in their praise of their patrons, whose vanity was often touched by what seems to us now the most inexcusable flattery. Dryden was no exception to his class, as the dedication of this poem shows.

The Duchess of Ormond was the daughter of Henry Beaufort, who was descended from John of Gaunt. She therefore had Plantagenet blood in her veins. Dryden dedicated his Book of Fables to the Duke of Ormond, and then added the special dedication of this poem to the Duchess.

Line 4. Chaucer's poem was so good as to make it doubtful whether he or Vergil deserved the palm.

7. *Ormond.* It is usual to speak of a nobleman in this way without prefixing his title of rank, but unusual to speak so of a peeress.

11. *Idea.* Ideal, *i. e.,* of womanhood.

15. *Princes* is the object of *made.*

18. *Noblest order.* The Order of the Garter. The story of the founding of that Order by Edward III. is that the Fair Maid of Kent, then the Countess of Salisbury, dropped her garter while dancing, and that the King, picking it up, put it on his own knee, saying: *Honi soit qui mal y pense.* (Evil to him who evil thinks).

29. *Platonic year.* The year in which the stars were supposed to return to the places from which they originally started. These years were supposed to occur after a period of about 26,000 years. The idea is that the Duchess of Ormond holds the same important place in the life of Dryden's time that the "fair Plantagenet" did in Chaucer's time.

31. *Fatal.* Fated. The house of Plantagenet is destined to be beautiful.

42. Grants of land in Ireland had been made to the Duke of Ormond. The Duke and the Duchess had accordingly gone to Ireland, the Duchess preceding her husband, as is indicated by line 54.

58. *Kerns.* The Irish name for light-armed infantry. V. *Macbeth,* Act I., Sc. 2.

59. *Hear the reins.* Imitation of Latin expression *audire habenas,* meaning to listen to and obey authority.

63. As the morning-star heralds the sun, so she heralded her husband's coming.

64. The battles of the Revolution of 1688 were fought in Ireland.

66. *One triumphant day.* The day of her arrival.

70. V. Genesis viii.

72. *Relics of mankind.* Noah and his family.

81. *Millenary year.* The millennium. The suggestion is that the coming of the Duchess is comparable to the coming of Christ. As her first coming cured the wounds of war, her second coming will cause the earth to bring forth crops without cultivation.

87. Some traditions have it that there never were reptiles in Ireland, others that St. Patrick destroyed them at an early day.

90. *This interval.* The Duchess had returned to England for a time.

99. *The dove.* The dove sent from Noah's ark.

107-10. Make the four lines the first half of a simile and supply the second half by giving the application of the thought to the Duchess.

117. *Four ingredients.* Earth, air, fire and water, the four elements of which the ancients thought the universe to be composed.

128. Had she died, Dryden, out of gratitude to her, would have written her elegy, though he would have detested the thought of her death.

130. The poem shows his vow to dedicate a poem to her as plainly as though it were a tablet on which the words of the vow were written.

138. It was less expensive for Heaven to preserve the Duchess than to make another woman of such exquisite parts.

139. *Middle science.* Between the knowledge of the physician and that of Heaven.

140. *Contingent.* Probable.

143. *Ormonds* is the object of *to hold.*

145. Is *may* the correct form after the past tense *meditated? Kind*, race family.

148. *First and last of each degree.* The highest and the lowest person in each class of society.

150. *The Graces.* The three goddesses of grace, beauty and joy, attend the Duchess when she is well. His power of song, that is, his Muse, has also come back to him.

152. *Red and white.* The red rose was the symbol of the House of Lancaster, the white of the House of York. The Duchess belonged to the House of Lancaster.

153. *Who* for *which*, referring to cheeks.

164. The Duchess had three daughters, but no son.

NOTES ON THE TEXT

Whenever the word, phrase or passage commented on is Dryden's a capital D is used after it; whenever it is Chaucer's, closely translated, a capital C is used; when Dryden translates Chaucer's thought freely no letter is used.

Comments on proper names are given in the Glossary.

ABBREVIATIONS.—V. vide; see or consult. Cf. confer; compare. Ded. Dryden's Dedication.

1-6. Notice the greater simplicity of Chaucer's wording. Pick out in Dryden's lines the phrases like *of mighty fame*, which have no parallel in Chaucer's. Scan l. 2. in each version for the pronunciation of Theseus.

12. D. Is the mixture of the figurative meaning of this line with the literal meaning of the next line artistic?

16-23. C. The events mentioned are the subject of the first book of Boccaccio's *Teseide;* as they are only indirectly related to the story of Palamon and Arcite, Chaucer shows his artistic sense by leaving them out.

30-33. C. A reference to the fact that the Canterbury pilgrims, at the suggestion of the host of the Tabard Inn, who went with them and acted as their guide, had promised a supper at the common cost to the one of their number who should tell the best story. Unfortunately the Canterbury Tales were never finished, and we consequently do not know which story the company liked best.

36. D. The knight is courteous enough to hope that some one else will tell a better story than his.

41. *Quire.* D. The same in derivation as our word choir; a company of people, not necessarily singers, and not limited to any definite number.

48. D. Is the line effective? What word spoils it?

50. *Weeds.* D. Originally not restricted to mourning. Look up its derivation.

56. *Swounded.* D. Swowned, C. Old forms of swooned.

57. *Nor.* Neither.

64. D. What is the effect of the Alexandrine?

69. Modern idiom would require "Thanks to Chance we were cast," etc. Cf. Chaucer's line. In both cases, what is the figure? Which line gives the figure more vividly?

71. Chaucer says definitely "a fourtenight."

79. *To make.* Making. *Have* is omitted before *lost;* what then is the construction of *rest*, l. 78, and *lords?*

81. D. Notice that Dryden's phrase is more condensed than Chaucer's.

94. *As.* As if.

98. *Crew.* D. A more general and dignified word in Dryden's time than now.

100. The knight's oath was to " protect the distressed, maintain right against might, and never by word or deed to stain his character as a knight or a Christian." V. article on Knights in International Cyclopedia.

109. *Argent.* D. Derivation? Notice that the word belongs to the science of heraldry, which had not been fully developed in Chaucer's time. For perfect construction, the clauses which follow *where* should be subordinate; *Where the God of War, Mars, was drawn . . with his . . . attire so aglow that the red light was reflected on the grass.*

115. *Pennon.* The ensign which all knights had a right to carry. It was often a narrow streamer, and was always pointed or forked at the end. The banner was a square ensign, borne before the king or leader in battle.

117. *Generous rage.* D. *Generous*, noble; *rage*, enthusiasm, zeal.

123. Here, again, Chaucer cuts out a whole book of the *Teseide.*

132. *Howling.* A notable instance of Dryden's occasional poor taste in the use of words; even Chaucer's word, "clamour," is not altogether pleasant.

138. D. What word in the sentence shows that *burned* must be a verb and not a participle?

142. *They.* Theseus's soldiers. **143.** *They.* Palamon and Arcite. *Sent* should be *had sent.* Was it natural that the young knights should be lying under the bodies of those whom they had killed?

141-54. What line in the passage tells something which Theseus's followers could not then have known? Does it weaken the description?

159. D. The expression is too condensed, because the ideas that the knights were found to belong to Creon's family, and that they were carefully nursed until they were well, are too unlike to belong in a single phrase. Technically, therefore, the sentence lacks unity of thought.

169. C. The first day of May, which Chaucer liked better than any other day in the year.

175. V. *Midsummer Night's Dream*, Act I, Sc. 1.

177. The observance of May-day used to be preceded in England by an all-night revel, in which every one shared.

197. *Sung.* In Dryden's day the form of the past tense in *u* was used where we now use the form in *a*. Notice the frequent examples in the poem.

204. D. The palace was a whole group of buildings, buil about a central open space. In this open court was the garden. The buildings, of which the tower was one, adjoined, making a continuous wall about the court. *Partition* is, therefore, used here in the sense of section.

214. D. Literal or derived meaning of *hateful*? Why is it an anachronism to speak of temples in Athens having spires?

232. D. Scan the line and notice that the break in rhythm serves to emphasize the thought. What does *inevitable* mean?

233. Love at first sight was the rule and not the exception, in times of chivalry. The knight chose his lady for her beauty without waiting to learn her disposition or character.

244. Both Chaucer and Dryden vacillate between the idea that the universe is ruled by God and the idea that it is ruled by Fate or Destiny. Dryden makes the idea of Fate rather more prominent than Chaucer does, but explains in lines 819-823 that he considers Fate is in accord with the will of God.

245. *Horoscope.* The diagram of the heavens at the

time of a person's birth, from which astrologers foretold the events of that person's life. V. Dictionary.

267. *Dungeon.* Astrologers divided the heavens into twelve "houses" by means of twelve great circles, intersecting the north and south poles of the heavens. Some of these houses were fortunate and some unfortunate in their influence. Saturn, the most unlucky planet, in the "dungeon of the sky," that is, the most unlucky house, would portend great evil.

272. *Fatal dart.* D. The reference is, of course, to the fact that Cupid, the god of love, wounds his victims with arrows sent from his golden bow.

282-310. What two points does Palamon make in arguing his own better right to Emily?

292. D. *That one should be*, etc. That each should share his good fortune with the other.

299. *On the plain.* D. In open fight.

300. *Appeach.* D. Impeach.

311-51. With what three points does Arcite reply to Palamon's two? Does he succeed in making the worse appear the better reason?

330. D. Love's power, which nature gives, is the sanction for any unfairness committed in the cause of love.

342-45. C. Is the simile an appropriate illustration? The full form would be, We plead our right as Æsop's hounds did when they contended. . . . but fruitlessly, for a cur, . . . Notice that l. 344-345 should be subordinate clauses.

382. D. Finds his purchase dear. Why?

383. *In prison pent.* D. Either, *I who was in prison pent*, or, *I who am still in prison pent*.

387. D. The condition of which l. 388 is the conclusion. What is the construction of *forced* ?

390. D. An example of the sacrifice of sense to rhyme. *Besides* is not merely unnecessary; it contradicts the idea already expressed.

399. *Adventure.* D. Chance for adventure or knightly deed.

400. D. Expand the metaphor into a simile.

404. D. What do poets mean by the not uncommon

phrase "Love's extremity"? Dryden's thought would have been well expressed by that phrase.

414. *And* for *nor*.

420-41. C. Arcite is enough of a philosopher to enjoy making a generalization from his own case.

427. *Guilty of their vows.* D. The Latin causal genitive. Guilty because they have broken their vows.

444-45. The false sequence of tense is Dryden's.

456. *Assemble ours.* D. Our forces. A Latinism.

457. Why would *avenge* be better than *vindicate?*

459. D. How would Emily be the *pledge of lasting peace?*

463. D. Effect of the Alexandrine?

474. *What.* In what.

483. D. Why is fortune called *giddy?*

484. D. *Our estate* (state) is worse than that of beasts.

485-96. A somewhat unfair argument, since the fact that man is capable of higher forms of pleasure than the beast is left out of the account.

493. *Forelays.* D. Waylays.

495. *Thrids.* D. Threads.

500. *A quartil.* D. An angle of 90 degrees. Planets at this angle were supposed to be at cross purposes, and, therefore, to cause trouble. · Notice that Mars represents jealousy and Venus love.

504. *By this.* D. By this time.

515. D. This playing upon words was thought in Dryden's time to add to the beauty of poetry. Pope, who followed Dryden both in time and method, carried the fashion to great extremes.

524-25. Dryden probably stated this idea in all seriousness as a physiological truth.

531. *Boxen.* D. An old adjective form. Of the box-tree.

537. *Swound.* Swoon.

538. *Deaf murmurs.* D. The thought is not very clear because two distinct, though similar, ideas are combined, namely that he hears sounds as though they were at a great distance, and that he hears sounds as mere murmurs, as a deaf person would.

539-42. Cf. Rosalind's description of the appearance of an ardent lover, in *As You Like It*, Act III. Sc. 2.

542. *Rage.* D. Madness.

550. *Sleep-compelling rod.* D. Notice the expressive phrase. V. Dictionary under caduceus.

554. Like the word of the gods given by oracles, the speech carries a hidden meaning; Arcite's death is hinted at.

576. Show that *conscious* is a poorly chosen word.

578. Is there any single adjective which could be substituted for *thick* ?

584. *Still.* Always.

590. *Philostratus.* The literal meaning from the Greek would be "fond of the army."

593-94. *Blown.* D. Another case where a poor word is chosen because of the rhyme.

601. D. Although he was only a menial at first.

602. D. *Largely entertained.* Liberally paid.

606. Grammatical error ?

BOOK II

620. *The Twins.* D. The sign of the zodiac called the Twins.

621. V. note on l. 244.

624. Chaucer says "the thridde (third) night."

644. *Style.* D. Pen. Derivation ?

651. *Tepid.* D. An unusual descriptive word.

661. *Against* in the sense of *toward* brings to mind Chaucer's lines about the daisy in the *Legende of Good Women.*

> —ther daweth[1] me no day
> That I nam[2] up, and walking in the mede
> To seen this flour agein[3] the sonne sprede.

668. *The sultry tropic.* D. The Tropic of Cancer, the northern limit of the sun's course. When the sun reaches that point the days are longest.

680. *But* for *than.*

692. C. Is the simile a happy one ?

694. Friday is named for Freya, the goddess of Northern mythology who corresponds to Venus.

---

[1]Dawneth. [2]Am not. [3]Against.

703. D. Cf. Æneid II, 325, *Fuit Ilium*.

713. *That side of heaven.* D. Jupiter and Juno did not always agree, and were leaders of two factions in the family of the gods. Mars and Vulcan sided with Juno, and Venus with Jupiter. Notice, as the story advances, how one *side of heaven* is interested for Palamon and the other for Arcite.

718. Was Palamon imprisoned because he was kin to Arcite?

722. D. "To fry" and "to hiss" are verbs often used by the poets of the seventeenth century to describe a lover's emotions.

723. D. Love is destroying him now, as Juno's hatred has before.

726. D. No goddess ever burned her temple, yet Emily burns his heart.

730. *His ears ring inward.* D. There is a ringing in his ears.

736. D. *Discovered* is used in its literal sense.

742. D. Cf. the meaning of *beguile* here with the meaning in l. 643.

757. C. Arcite renounces all his early pledges of friendship.

760. Notice the substantive use of the adjective.

763. D. Expand the metaphor in *titles* to a simile.

771. D. Does the line add to the effect of the passage, or detract from it?

775. Each had left his promise to be redeemed.

791. C. State the full simile.

792. D. *Hopes.* Hopes for, awaits.

798. *Generous chillness.* D. Noble coolness or courage.

806. *Foin.* D. Thrust.

817. Notice the broken construction; *and make the forest ring*, etc., would have carried out the structure consistently.

824-31. One would think that Dryden had been studying Calvinism had not Chaucer expressed a similar thought.

838. *Lively green.* D. Cf. "living green," a common phrase in modern poetry.

845. *Laund.* C. Etymologically the same as lawn, but meaning a glade, *i. e.,* an open space in the wood.

851. *Looking underneath the sun.* C. Perhaps means definitely that he looked toward the east.

854. *Fauchions.* Falchions.

869. *Unasked the royal grant.* D. Is the use of the nominative absolute to express a condition common in English ?

879. Scan.

902. D. Supply *is.*

909. V. Chaucer's lines. Neither version credits Palamon with an ideal spirit, but in which is he less magnanimous ?

924. *The contended maid, i. e.* Emily. D. In modern English the passive voice of this verb is not used with a personal subject.

926-33. D. Chaucer has no parallel lines.

928. *Mastership.* D. Masterpiece.

930. *They, i. e.,* the wounds.

937. *Grace.* D. Forgiveness.

948. *He . . . he.* Palamon . . . Theseus.

950. *Under.* D. Down. Notice that the phrase "to look down with the eyes" follows the Latin rather than the Englism idiom.

962. D. Borrowed from the classic poets, who often speak of Jove's "awful nod." The implication is that Love is as powerful as Jove.

971. *In their own despite.* D. Why is it more logical to understand the phrase here as meaning *to their own disadvantage* rather than *in spite of themselves ?*

981. *Ask.* D. If you ask.

991. D. Grammatical inaccuracy ?

1008. *Both.* Both of you. Why, *but too well ?*

1018. *Every sign, i. e.,* of the Zodiac. D. When the sun has finished his yearly course.

1023. Give him such success that he shall drive his foe out of the lists.

1025. *Recreant.* D. Yielding or cowardly.

1031. D. *Of* is the objective genitive; Theseus will be the patron for both knights.

1055. *Degrees.* C. Steps.

1057. The pitch was steep enough for one person to see over the head of the person in front of him.

1072. Why was it appropriate that the Temple of Mars should be opposite that of Venus?

1077. Notice that an *oratory* is primarily a place of prayer.

1078. *Imagery.* D. The word is usually applied to the rhetorical figures of prose or poetry; here it means images or statues.

1080. *Addressed.* D. Sacred or dedicated.

1080-1100. What, in Dryden's picture, could be painted and what could not?

1093. *Sigils.* D. Seals on which were stamped signs of the planets when in some lucky position. They were sometimes worn as talismen.

1097-99. *Suffused.* D. Probably with color. What two words suggest the color yellow? Chaucer says that jealousy wore a garland of yellow marigolds. The cuckoo is the symbol of deception, perhaps because it lays its eggs in another bird's nest.

1099. Either *down-looked* is the verb for all the nouns beginning with *beauty* and *and* is superfluous, or the verb *were* is to be supplied from 1097 and *down-looked* means *down-looking.*

1107. D. Chaucer is less careful to defend himself against the charge of anachronism in giving the examples which follow.

1119-20. Supply *that* to make the clauses correspond in construction with those that precede.

1129. *Buxom.* D. Flexible, pliant.

1130. V. glossary, under Cupid.

1146. *Knares.* C. Guarls.

1149. How far should the relative clause extend?

1150. D. Imperfect rhyme, and shifting of tenses.

1154. *Bent.* C. Slope.

1155-69. Among other objects represented in this picture on the wall of the oratory of Mars was a Temple of Mars.

1159. *Blind.* D. Not admitting light.

1170-1226. It is best to understand this passage as describing the rest of the paintings on the walls of the oratory, although both Chaucer and Dryden go on with the description as though they might still be speaking of the Temple of Mars which appears in one of the paintings. Notice that throughout the passage the influence of the planet Mars is confused with that of Mars, the god of war.

1178. D. What is the underlying thought of the line?

1182. *Lawn.* D. Another subject of *stood.*

1187. *Clottered.* D. Clotted.

1202. *Mars his nature.* In Dryden's time the apostrophe *s* was thought to be a broken down and incorrect form of the possessive pronoun. V. also l. 1214.

1210. *Scarlet conquest.* A figure representing Conquest in a scarlet robe. Is the figure of Victory usually that of a man or woman?

1217. Dryden's clause, *Who lost the world for love*, is out of place here, since it suggests that the picture of Antony belongs in the Temple of Venus.

1218. *Fane.* D. Derivation?

1221. Does Mars really look redder than the other planets?

1224. "To form geomantic figures, proceed thus: Take a pencil and hurriedly jot down on a paper a number of dots in a line, without counting them. Do the same three times more. Now count the dots, to see whether they are odd or even. If the dots in a line are odd, put one dot on another small paper, half-way across it. If they are even, put down *two* dots, one towards each side, arranging the results in four rows, one beneath the other." (From Mr. W. W. Skeat's Notes on the Canterbury Tales.)

Mr. Skeats gives the figures Puella and Rubeus thus:

```
    *                    *    *
 *     *                   *
    *                    *    *
    *                    *    *
```

There were sixteen of these geomantic figures, each with its name, its element, its planet and its sign, and the astrologers sometimes made their divinations from these figures instead of taking the actual position of the stars. Geomancy was sometimes called "divination by spotting," and was a sort of abbreviated astrology; the figures were made at first by throwing pebbles carelessly upon the ground (γῆ), from which the science took its name.

1226. D. A planet is *direct* when it appears to move from west to east with the signs of the Zodiac, and *retrograde* when it appears to move from east to west.

1230. *Shades.* D. Of trees.

1233. *Manifest of shame.* D. A Latinism, meaning *with shame manifest*.

1235. *Peculiar grace.* D. Jupiter was especially merciful in placing the mother and the son near each other.

1236. *In the cold circle.* D. The Arctic circle.

1239. What should we say instead of *unknowing of?*

1243-44. The next wall-painting showed the Greeks assembled in a temple, and the next showed them in pursuit of the boar sent by Diana to ravage Calydon. There is no connection between the lines, except possibly that the Greeks prayed to Diana before they started on the hunt; but that idea is scarcely logical, since it was Diana's wish that the boar should punish Œneus for his slight to her.

1249. *The Volscian Queen.* D. Camilla, V. Glossary under Camilla.

1259. *Wexing.* C. Waxing, growing.

1260. Why is the moon's light called *borrowed?*

1262. *Alternate sway.* Diana was confused by the Romans with Hecate, the goddess of night and the world of spirits, and also with Persephone, wife of Pluto. From l. 1489 it appears that Dryden confuses her with Persephone, and means that she rules in Hades part of the year. Notice that the planet and the goddess are confused.

1271-72. D. Notice how the unity of the passage is broken by these two lines, which drop out of the particular past time into an indefinite present time.

Book III

1279. *Round the world.* D. Chaucer has no parallel phrase.

1290. *The fair.* D. The fair sex.

1292. *Not scarce.* Modern use drops the *not.*

1311. *Jambeux.* Jambeaux. From French, *jambe,* the leg.

1322. Unity of construction would require the phrase "round and long of arm," in place of the clause.

1337. *His* only in the sense that they were Palamon's, and that after Palamon himself he led Palamon's forces.

1365. *Reclaimed.* D. Tamed, trained.

1366. *His.* In reality Arcite's.

1377. *War.* Troops. Metonymy.

1379. *Sunday.* C. A startling anachronism.

1384. By the change of what one word might the change in subject and in voice have been avoided?

1389. *How.* To what lady.

1392. Construction of the nouns *sighs* and *love?*

1400. *Preventing.* D. Used in its literal sense; *prevenire,* to go before.

1407. *Sliding.* D. Probably used in allusion to the ancient idea that each of the heavenly bodies was set in its own crystalline sphere, and that all these spheres "slid" around each other in the heavens, with the earth as a center. The Sun was in the fourth of these spheres and Venus in the third; therefore, Venus was nearer the earth, or *beneath* the Sun.

1408. *Become,* for consistency, should be *becomest.*

1410. *Thy month.* May.

1417. *Gladder.* C. Thou who dost make glad.

1418. *Increase of Jove.* Daughter of Jove. Companion of the Sun because Venus is the morning star.

1440. *Fifth.* A mistake for third.

1441. *Clue.* Thread. Palamon makes no reference to the Fates in Chaucer's version.

1444. *Cut below your line.* D. Let the Fates cut off the thread of my life before I am without love, for I prefer to live a short time with love rather than a long time without it. Express in a simile the comparison implied by the metaphors of this passage through line 1446.

1457. D. Palamon took the fact that the flame was so slow in coming as a sign that he must wait a long time for the fulfillment of his prayer.

1465. *Vests.* D. Vestments.

1480. *Mastless.* Without acorns.

1494. *Feathered deaths.* D. Feathered arrows. What figure?

1501. *Servant.* Lover.

1504. Diana was the goddess of the moon, of the chase, and, as Persephone, of Hades. V. note on 1. 1262.

1519. D. Tell why this line is inappropriate.

1520-21. What rhetorical fault in the lines?

1522. This first *burning fire* means Palamon, the *victor-flame* in l. 1526 means Arcite. Trace the fulfillment of this prophecy as you read the rest of the poem.

1528. Literal meaning of *irrevocable?*

1541. *The rest.* As for the rest.

1546. D. Incoherent construction ; *unwilling* should limit *gods* and *doomed* should limit *thee.*

1549. *Which the man, i. e.,* who is to win ? *Thunderer,* Jupiter.

1556. *Disclaimed.* D. Deserted by Diana. Therefore she is no longer *a sister of the wood, i. e.,* one of Diana's followers.

1562-63. The seven planets that were supposed to control the destiny of man were the Sun, the Moon, and Saturn, Jupiter, Mars, Venus, and Mercury. Each hour in the day was said to be controlled by one of these planets. V. Skeat's Chaucer, Vol. V., p. 86.

1579-82. D. To what lines in the early part of the poem does this passage refer ?

1585. Nor has Mars forgotten his own pain when he was a lover himself.

1587. Cf. l. 1417.

1598. *Unpractised to persuade.* D. What is the modern idiom ?

1601. *Or.* Either.

1607. *For.* For the sake of.

1629. *Close.* D. Enclosed space. What is the usual meaning of the noun ?

1653. *Leaden.* D. In astrology, lead was the metal which was thought best to indicate the influence of Saturn.

1660. A blind line, which is perhaps a mistranslation of Chaucer's. Age may be outrun by youth, but not surpassed in good counsel.

1661-62. D. Venus and Saturn were 120 degrees (a trine) apart, and Saturn obscured (*i.e.*, gulled), Mars. Therefore Saturn and Venus would work together and overcome Mars.

1663. *In his own abode.* D. In the same sign of the zodiac.

1666. C. Saturn promises to answer both the prayer of Palamon and the prayer of Arcite.

1673. Three signs of the zodiac were " watery," three "earthy," three " fiery," and three " airy." When Saturn is in a " watery " sign, he wrecks ships, etc.

1680. When he speaks of the " cherles rebellynge," Chaucer is probably thinking of Jack Straw's rebellion. When Dryden speaks of churls who *rebel against their native prince,* he may easily be thinking of the Revolution of 1688 which drove James II. from the throne.

1682. Who is *housing ?* A misrelated participle.

1694. *Complexions.* C. Temperaments. Medieval physiology taught that there were four temperaments, the choleric, the sanguine, the phlegmatic and the melancholic.

1703. According to l. 1379 this day was Monday.

1711-14. D.

1747. Emetrius.

1750. Lycurgus.

1761. *Cap-a-pe.* Cap-a-pie. French for " from head to foot."

1766. Who did the *signing ?* Another misrelated participle.

1769. *Bespeaks.* D. Speaks to; a poetic use only. What is the prose meaning ?

1770. *In his mind.* D. A Latinism.

1774. *Rebate.* D. Abate.

1788. *At mischief.* C. At disadvantage.

1790. *Captives made.* If made captives they cannot again enter the fight.

1792. *Chief of either side.* Palamon or Arcite.

1796. *Vaulted firmament.* The throne of l. 1759 must, then, have been out of doors, perhaps in the court of the palace.

1814. *Southern gate.* The other three gates were perhaps less accessible because of the three temples.

1824. *The guards.* Object of *overbear.*

1831. *Divides the plain.* D. Takes his half of the lists.

1837. Appropriateness of the word *shares?*

1841. *Sized.* Matched.

1842. Literal meaning of *nice?*

1844. Grammatically *ranged* limits *herald;* what should it limit to express the thought?

1855. *In the rest.* C. In the rest at the side of the saddle, ready for action.

1861. *Shock.* D. Come together.

1879. *This.* This knight.

1901. Who was the *tiger* and who the *lion?* V. l. 812.

1914. *He.* Emetrius struck Palamon.

1922. Construction of *o'erpowered?*

1928. *Hateful.* Full of hate, V. l. 214.

1941. V. Glossary under Cronus.

1947. *Her will refused.* What word must be supplied to make the expression correspond in form with the clause connected to it by *and?*

1950. *The blustering fool.* D. Mars.

1952. Scan the line, noticing the elision in *th'arrears.* The elision is rare in Dryden, but very frequent in Chaucer. Indeed, Chaucer sometimes runs the two words together in spelling as well as in sound. V. *Th'effect,* footnote on l. 1560.

The arrears (D) means the unfulfilled promise of Venus to Palamon.

1963. *Endlong.* C. Headlong.

1969-70. Another instance of Dryden's fashion of breaking the unity of a passage to make a general comment.

1976. *Quivered with his feet.* D. Cf. Latin ablative of specification.

1992. *Compelled.* D. Notice the literal meaning; *compellere*, to drive together.

1993. How may it be determined from the structure of the sentence that *composed* is a verb, and not a participle?

1996. Notice the omission of the principal verb. In prose, the full form, *was the fact that none were slain*, would be necessary.

2010. Another elliptical expression. *It proves only that the victor*, etc.

2021. *Impairs.* D. Is impaired.

2027. *Breathing reins.* Blood-letting.

2031. *Bellows.* Is the metaphor a happy one? Why not?

2044. *Against right.* Is this the first time that Arcite acknowledges that he is in the wrong?

2057. *Officious.* The literal meaning from *officiosus;* ready to serve. What is the meaning now?

2058. *Excuse my faltering tongue,* (which cannot tell you) *how I have loved.*

2060-65. What words would have to be differently placed in prose?

2069. Notice how entirely unspiritual Arcite's idea of death is.

2078. Why does Arcite call Emily his foe?

2090. Derivation of *concurrent?*

2102. D. We have often proved our affection for each other.

2109. *Below.* Upon his limbs.

2110-11. *He.* Death.

2112-16. *He.* Arcite.

2117. *Who.* What word does modern idiom require after *such?*

2116-25. How much does this passage add to the story of Arcite? It is freely translated from Chaucer, and enlarged.

2129. *Her lover's.* Arcite's.

2135. D. The idea is not clearly expressed. *It* probably refers to *sorrow*, l. 2132.

2142. *But Hector was not then.* The time of this story is supposed to precede that of the Trojan war.

2147-54. A very loosely constructed sentence. *Ægeus* is the antecedent of *who, altering* limits *fate, good* and *delight* are in apposition with *vicissitudes.*

2155-62. These are the ideas that Ægeus expresses.

2164. D. The line is inartistic, not only because it introduces an idea foreign to the subject, but also because it gives an exaggerated idea of the fickleness of mankind.

2177. *Sere-wood.* Dry wood.
Doddered. Decayed, and covered with a vine called dodder.

2180. *Vulcanian food.* Fuel, the food of fire, of which Vulcan was the god. V. Glossary.

2197. D. The hair, which was worn in long flowing locks, was considered by the ancients a sacred offering. V. 1. 1623.

2198. *Chief.* Chief mourner.

2204. *Atchievements.* Accoutrements.

2212. *The master-street.* C. The principal street. Old cities had a chief street which was to the others what the spinal cord is to the nervous system of the body.

2225. D. The pile was so high that even a bow made by the Parthians, the best bowmen of the time, could not send an arrow to the top of it.

2232. D. Spear shafts were made of the wood of the ash.

2233-34. Prove the appropriateness of the epithets.

2237. Unity of construction would demand, *and what the nymphs were called* (shall rest untold). The nymphs that lived in trees were called dryads.

2239. *Nor. And* would be better, with the negative *untold* in the predicate.

2240. *Disherited.* D. Disinherited. When a tree was destroyed the dryad who lived in it was left without a home.

2244. *Stranger* is in apposition with *ground.*

2296. *Cause and Spring of motion.* The Creator.

2299. D. The *jarring seeds* were fire, water, earth and air, usually called the elements, from which the whole universe was supposed to have sprung. The ancients thought that these elements warred with each other during the first period of the creation, which they called Chaos.

2311. *Suborn.* D. Usually said of a witness who is hired to testify falsely in a law court. The idea is that they are dealing unfairly by putting an end to their lives before the appointed time has come.

2322. *The ethereal fire.* D. The soul.

2323. D. Man's *mortal part* decays, and is taken up again by the earth. It is interesting to notice that Dryden had this idea, which has been so greatly developed by modern science; but it is doubtful whether this expression of the thought in a speech which is supposed to give consolation for the death of Arcite is very artistic.

2345. D. He grudges his parents their authority.

2349. *Rich of three souls.* D. Rich in having three souls. The medieval conception was that a person had three souls, the vegetive, which controlled the unconscious plant-like life of the body, the sensitive, which controlled the conscious life of the senses, and the rational, which controlled the mind. These souls developed one after the other.

2350. D. Some, who live long enough to develop all three souls, merely waste their lives; but thousands more die before the "rational soul" has been developed.

2352. *First.* D. First stage of life, when only the vegetive soul has been developed.

2371. *Joy us of.* Congratulate us upon.

2381. D. *On him* (their sorrow) *is lost.*

2408. D. Emily gives her hand to Theseus.

GLOSSARY

Actaeon. l. 258. A famous huntsman, who saw Artemis (Diana) while she was bathing, and was changed by her into a stag. His own hounds pursued and killed him.

Adonis. l. 1419. The beautiful youth whom Venus loved. While hunting, he was killed by a boar.

Ægeus. l. 2149. One of the early kings of Athens, and the father of Theseus.

Æsop. l. 342. The author of a large number of fables which teach practical lessons by the conversation of animals. The tradition is, that Æsop was a slave, who lived in Phrygia about 600 B. C.

Amazons. l. 17. A mythical race of women-warriors, who lived north of the Black Sea, and who were the subject of many legends. Both Hercules and Theseus were said to have fought with and subdued them.

Antony. l. 1217. Mark Antony, with Lepidus and Octavius Caesar, formed the second triumvirate. At Actium he defeated his own cause by withdrawing from the battle to follow Cleopatra's ship. As a consequence, Octavius became Emperor of Rome. V. *Antony and Cleopatra*, Act III., Sc. 10 and 11.

Apollo. l. 1242. Son of Zeus and brother of Artemis. He was the god of light and music. He loved the nymph Daphne.

Arcite. Chaucer pronounced the name Ar-sē'-te, Dryden, Ar'-sīte or Ar-sīte'. Chaucer's pronunciation is in best accord with Greek pronunciation.

Argus. l. 552. A giant, who had eyes all over his head and body. Hermes, at Zeus' command, put all the eyes to sleep by using his caduceus and flute, and then beheaded the monster.

Ascanius. Ded l. 162. Also called Iulus; the son of Æneas.

Atalanta. l. 1246. The fleet-footed maiden who first touched the boar in the Calydonian hunt, and to whom Meleager accordingly gave the "envied prize" of the boar's head and skin. Meleager's love for her led him to kill his uncles; hence the "fatal power of Atalanta's eyes." V. Œnides.

Athens. l. 5. The capital of Attica, and the most famous city of Greece. Tradition says that Theseus gave the city a constitutional government and laid the foundation of its greatness.

Aurora. l. 186. Goddess of dawn. She is said by the poets to ride in her chariot, which is drawn by the swift horses Lampus and Phaeton, along the stream of Ocean and up to Heaven, to announce to the gods first and then to mortals that the light of day is about to appear.

Bacchus. l. 1375. Called by the Greeks Dionysus. He was the god of wine, song and revelry, and was pictured as followed by a train of both men and animals. He went even to India to introduce vine-culture.

Cadmus. l. 703. The legendary hero who built the citadel of Thebes. Before doing so he slew the dragon which Mars (Ares) had sent to guard the place, and thus incurred the hatred of Mars and Juno.

Caesar. l. 1215. Caius Julius Caesar, Roman consul, general and dictator, was assassinated in the capitol at Rome March 15th (the Ides) 44 B.C. A soothsayer warned him not to go to the capitol that day. V. Plutarch's *Lives* and Shakspere's *Julius Caesar*, Act II., Sc. 2.

Calisto or Callisto. l. 1233. A nymph of Artemis (Diana), who was punished for a crime by being changed to a bear. She was slain by Artemis, and became a star in the constellation of the Bear. Her son was placed beside her in the constellation.

Calydonia. l. 1244. A city and region in Ætolia. Homer speaks of the beauty and fertility of the plain of "lovely" Calydon.

Camilla. l. 1249. Queen of the Volscians, and a votress of Diana. In Æneas's war against the Volscians one of his followers, Aruns, killed Camilla. Diana avenged Camilla's death by causing the death of Aruns.

Capaneus. l. 76. One of the Seven Against Thebes. (V. Thebes.) He was scaling the wall, boasting that even a thunderbolt from Zeus should not keep him from entering the city, when Zeus slew him with a thunderbolt. His wife's name was Evadne. (V. l. 55.)

Ceres. Ded l. 65. The goddess of harvest and agriculture.

Circe. l. 1115. An enchantress into whose hands Odysseus fell on his way home from the Trojan war. In order to detain Odysseus she gave part of his crew drugged wine and turned them into beasts.

Citheron. l. 1108. Dryden probably meant Cythe'ra, an island near Crete, from which the worship of Aphrodite (Venus) was carried to Greece. Possibly the reference is to a range of mountains in Greece, called Cithaeron; but these mountains were especially consecrated to Zeus and Dionysus.

Creon. l. 81. Called by Sophocles the "Tyrant of Thebes." (V. Thebes.) He was the uncle of Antigone, Polynices and Eteocles. His refusal to let Antigone bury her brother, who had fallen in the expedition of the Seven Against Thebes, is the subject of Sophocles's *Antigone.* The complaint of the widows of the other leaders of that expedition, given in l. 55-88, is the occasion of Theseus's marching on Thebes. Theseus conquered the city and put Creon to death.

Cronus. l. 1698. Sometimes, though less correctly, spelled Chronus. The son of Uranus (Heaven) and Gaea (Earth), and the father of Zeus. He overthrew his father, placed himself on the throne and thus established the second dynasty of the gods; but he was overthrown in turn by his son, Zeus, who established the third dynasty. The Romans identified Cronus with Saturn, whom they considered the great compromiser among the gods.

Cupid. l. 1130. The son of Venus and the god of love. He is represented as a winged boy, carrying a golden bow and a golden quiver full of arrows. Whoever he hit with an arrow was overcome with the power of love.

Cynthia. l. 1231. The name given to Artemis from Mt. Cynthus, in the Island of Delos, where she was born. The name was afterwards applied by the Romans to Diana, whom they identified with Artemis.

Cyprus. l. 261. The same as the modern Cyprus. Aphrodite (Venus) was said to have been born on the island, and was therefore called the Cyprian Queen.

Elisa. Ded. l. 162. Dido, Queen of Carthage.

Daphne. l. 1241. A nymph, daughter of the river-god Peneus. When Apollo pursued her she prayed to Artemis to save her from his love, and Artemis changed her into a laurel tree.

Diana. l. 1223. The Roman goddess who corresponded to the Greek Artemis. She was the deity of the moon, the chase and the forest.

Etesian. Ded. l. 46. From ἔτος, a year. Periodical winds, especially the favorable north winds which blew on the Ægean for forty days after the rising of the dog-star.

Fates. l. 1441. (Ded. 40.) Also called Moerae or Moirae, and Parcae. They were sisters; Clotho spun the thread of life. Lachesis determined how long it should be, and Atropos cut it off. They are sometimes represented as deciding the fates both of gods and of men, sometimes as subject to the will of Zeus.

Graces. Ded. l. 150. The three goddesses of grace, beauty and joy.

Hector. l. 2142. Son of Priam, King of Troy. He was the leader of the Trojans when the Greeks besieged the city and his fall led to the victory of the Greeks.

Hermes. l. 547. Called by the Romans Mercury, the messenger of the gods, and especially of Zeus. He was also the god of dreams, and his wand, the caduceus, was "sleep-compelling."

Hibernia. Ded l. 53. The Latin name for Ireland.

Hippolyta. l. 7. The Queen of the Amazons whom Theseus married after conquering her followers.

Idalia. l. 1108. The name of a forest and town in Cyprus sacred to Aphrodite (Venus); there is no mention of a mountain near the place.

Jove or Jupiter. l. 759. (Ded. 133.) Called by the Greeks Zeus. He was the king of gods and men and his will was supreme. He was called the Thunderer because, as king of heaven, he controlled the powers of the air, and hurled the thunderbolts.

Juno. l. 260. Called by the Greeks Hera. She was the wife of Jupiter, and queen of the gods.

Lycurgus. l. 1315. There was a king of Thrace by this name who was said to have expelled Dionysus from his kingdom. Probably, however, Chaucer had no definite person in mind.

Mars. l. 500. The god of war He is the son of Juno and corresponds to the Greek god Ares.

Macedon, The. Ded. l. 133. Alexander the Great, King of Macedon, the country north of Greece.

Medea. l. 1115. The daughter of the King of Colchis, and an enchantress. By her charms she helped Jason to get the golden fleece.

Minotaur. 1. 116. The Bull of Minos, a monster with the head of a bull and the body of a man. He was hid in the labyrinth of Crete, and fed on youths and maidens, sent as tribute from Athens, until Theseus, with Ariadne's help, penetrated the labyrinth and slew him.

Morley. Ded. 1. 131. Dr. Morley was physician to the Duchess of Ormond.

Narcissus. 1. 1112. A beautiful youth, the son of a river god, who rejected the love of the nymph Echo. Aphrodite punished him by making him fall in love with his own face, reflected in a pool. He pined away and died because he could not withdraw his eyes from the reflection.

Nereids. Ded. 1. 45. Sea-nymphs, daughters of the sea-god Nereus.

Niobe. 1. 1494. Wife of Amphion, King of Thebes. She boasted that she was superior to Leto because she had six sons and six daughters while Leto had only two children, Apollo and Artemis. As punishment, Leto had Apollo and Artemis kill all of Niobe's children with their arrows.

Œnides. 1. 1245. Meleager. The form Œnides is a patronymic from Œneus. Œneus, King of Calydonia, offended Artemis by forgetting to offer sacrifice to her. She accordingly sent a boar to ravage his country. His son Meleager, who was a famous Greek hero and who had been a member of the Argonautic expedition, called together a number of Greek warriors to hunt the boar. They killed it, but Artemis, in revenge, stirred up a quarrel among them about the possession of the boar's skin.

Meleager gave the prize to Atalanta, and slew his mother's brothers for trying to steal it from her. Meleager's mother had received a prophecy that her son should live as long as a brand which was on the hearth when he was born, remained unconsumed. Angered at the murder of her brothers, she threw this brand upon the fire, and her son died when the brand was consumed.

Ormond, Duchess of. Ded. Title. Daughter of Henry Beaufort, a descendant of John of Gaunt, the son of Edward Third.

Pales. Ded. 1. 65. The deity of cattle and pastures.

Parthia. 1. 2225. A wild country of indefinite extent in western Asia, east of the Caspian Sea.

Penelope. Ded. 1. 158. The wife of Ulysses. During Ulysses's ten years' absence at the Trojan war she put off her suitors with the excuse that she could not marry until she had finished a certain piece of embroidery. She embroidered during the day time and pulled out her work at night.

Philomel. 1. 199. The daughter of a king of Attica, who was changed into a nightingale.

Phospher. 1. 1396. The bringer of light. The name was given to Venus when she appeared as the morning star.

Pirithous, or Peirithous. 1. 358. A prince of Thessaly.

Plantagenet. Ded. 1. 30. The line of kings of whom Henry Second was the first. They ruled in England from 1154-1485, and were, consequently, the ruling family in Chaucer's time. The "Fairest Plantagenet" was Joan, "The Fair Maid of Kent," granddaughter of Edward First. She was married three times; her second husband was the Earl of Salisbury, and her third the Black Prince, son of Edward Third.

Pluto. 1. 1972. Son of Cronus and brother of Zeus and Poseidon. He was the ruler of Hades, and was called Hades in Greek mythology.

Portunus. Ded. 1. 48. The god of ports and harbors.

Pruce. 1. 1307. Prussia.

Ptolemy. Ded. 1. 134. A general of Alexander the Great. He afterwards became King of Egypt.

Samson. 1. 1113. One of the Judges of the Children of Israel, known in sacred history as the "strongest man." He lost his strength when, at the solicitation of Delilah, he broke his vow. V. Judges xvi. 4-21.

Saturn. V. Cronus.

Scythia. 1. 7. A wild, uninhabited region of indefinite extent in eastern Europe and western Asia. In later times the name was applied more definitely to the country north of the Black Sea.

Solomon. 1. 1113. The son of David and King of Israel at the time of that nation's greatest prosperity. His heart was turned from God because he loved " many strange women." V. 1 Kings xi. 1-5.

Statius. 1. 1484. A Latin poet who lived in Naples in the first century A.D. His chief poem was the *Thebaid*, a poem in twelve books, which told the stories of the seven heroes who besieged Thebes under the leadership of Polynices. (V. Thebes.)

Thebes. 1. 77. The most famous city in Grecian mythology. When Œdipus fled from Thebes after the discovery that he had murdered his father, his sons Eteocles and Polynices succeeded him.

They quarreled, and Polynices departed from the city to gather allies. Six heroes joined him, among them Capaneus, and the expedition has come to be famous, as the subject of Aeschylus's tragedy *The Seven Against Thebes*.

Theseus. 1. 2. One of the favorite legendary heroes of Greece. The stories about him tell how he went on the Argonautic expedition, how he slew the Minotaur, conquered the Amazons, took part in the Calydonian hunt and established the government of Athens. But there is no historical proof that such a person as Theseus ever lived. It is interesting to notice that Shakspere represents the revel of *Midsummer Night's Dream* as taking place at the nuptials of Theseus and Hippolyta.

Thrace. 1. 1137. A large country north of Greece, of about the same extent as modern Turkey. It was a wild, mountainous region, inhabited by barbarous tribes, and thought by the Greeks to be forbiddingly cold.

Titan. 1. 1941. The oldest son of Heaven and Earth, and oldest brother of Cronus. When he and his offspring, the Titans, tried to get the throne of Heaven from Cronus, Zeus overcame them and cast them down to Tartarus.

Triton. Ded. 1. 44. The Tritons were the sons of Poseidon, the god of the sea.

Troy. 1. 2141. The chief city of Troas, in ancient Asia Minor. Paris, son of Priam, King of Troy and younger brother of Hector, visited Greece and carried off Helen, the wife of Menelaus, King of Sparta. Menelaus and his brother, Agamemnon, led the Greeks against Troy, and the siege lasted ten years. The story of the war is told in Homer's Iliad.

Venus. 1. 262. The daughter of Jupiter. She is the Roman deity corresponding to the Greek Aphrodite. She was the goddess of love and the mother of Cupid. Her symbol was the dove.

Vespasian. Ded 1. 125. Titus, the son of the Emperor Vespasian. His siege of Jerusalem was one of the most famous and one of the most horrible events in history. He was said to have wept when he saw the Temple of Jerusalem in flames.

Vulcan. The sun of Jupiter and Juno, corresponding to the Greek Hephaestus. He was the husband of Venus. As the artificer among the gods he is represented at his anvil, where, among other things, he forges the thunderbolts of Jupiter.

INDEX

Page references are to the introduction; line references, to the poem. Notes on the passages referred to, should also be consulted.

www.ingramcontent.com/pod-product-compliance
Lightning Source LLC
Chambersburg PA
CBHW020231030726
47497CB00009B/3045